"Are you offering me five million dollars to sleep with you?"

His eyes narrowed. "The point is, would you?"

Briar opened her mouth to shout, *No!* And then she stifled her anger.

"It's a high price to pay," she said huskily.

A leaping flame seemed to come and go in his eyes. "Don't you think you're worth it?"

DAPHNE CLAIR lives in Aotearoa, New Zealand, with her Dutch-born husband. Their five children have left home, but drift back at irregular intervals. At eight years old she embarked on her first novel, about taming a tiger. This epic never reached a publisher, but metamorphosed male tigers still prowl the pages of her romances. Her other writing includes non-fiction, poetry and short stories. And she has won literary prizes in both New Zealand and America.

Books by Daphne Clair

HARLEQUIN PRESENTS
1586—AND THEN CAME MORNING
1648—FLAME ON THE HORIZON
1688—DARK MIRROR

DAPHNE CLAIR

Infamous Bargain

Harlequin Books

TORONTO • NEW YORK • LONDON
AMSTERDAM • PARIS • SYDNEY • HAMBURG
STOCKHOLM • ATHENS • TOKYO • MILAN
MADRID • WARSAW • BUDAPEST • AUCKLAND

ISBN 0-373-11730-2

INFAMOUS BARGAIN

Copyright © 1994 by Daphne Clair de Jong.

First North American Publication 1995.

Printed in U.S.A.

CHAPTER ONE

BRIAR slipped a pair of long silver and garnet earrings into place and rearranged a tendril of hair that had fallen against her cheek.

The deceptively casual style suited her, and the 'Sunset' rinse she'd had last week added a touch of warmth to what she thought of as a rather insipid colour. In her teenage years the extreme fairness of childhood had given way to something between brown and blonde. The rinse wasn't obvious. Her father had cast it a puzzled, cursory glance, and apparently dismissed the subtle change as a figment of his imagination.

She could hear his voice, rich and a trace over-hearty, greeting the arriving guests. Already the doorbell had rung three or four times. Her stepmother would be in a flutter as usual, nervously checking impeccable place-settings, twitching unnecessarily at cushions, and darting out to the kitchen to ensure the caterers were coping, although they were from one of Auckland's best and most experienced firms.

Briar checked her make-up. The new 'Tropic Dusk' eyeshadow was a subtle shade, making eyes that were neither blue nor grey seem larger, darker and somehow mysterious. Better go down. Laura would need her calming presence, and her father would be getting impatient if she didn't soon appear and start being polite and welcoming to the financiers and lawyers and business people exchanging small talk over glasses of imported whisky and gold-medal New Zealand wines.

'And I want you to pay special attention to Kynan Roth,' he'd instructed Briar. 'Make sure he has a good time.'

He hadn't noticed the ironic glance that his daughter threw at him, and she'd bitten her tongue on the remark that hovered on the tip of it. Xavier Cunningham, despite his experience in business and his assiduous cultivation of the well-to-do and the financially useful, was probably totally unaware that his twenty-four-year-old daughter was capable of even slightly ribald thoughts. Briar knew very well that all he was asking of her was to act the poised, gracious hostess that his second wife had never learned to be.

Briar slid a pair of high-heeled pumps over her gossamer-stockinged feet, and adjusted the thin straps of the sheer floating confection of champagne chiffon over silk that she'd bought for tonight. Her father had insisted on her having a new dress, and even provided a hefty cheque for it.

She walked along the brass-edged carpet laid between gleaming kauri boards along the wide upstairs hall, and paused at the top of the curved staircase. The old, proudly preserved mansion, set in half an acre of mature garden in the long-established suburb of Remuera, was an estate agent's dream. A Persian rug on the floor of the high-ceilinged lobby deadened the footsteps of the middle-aged couple her father was ushering into the big living-room from which a babble of voices floated. As the bell burred once more he inclined his handsome greying head and said to them, 'I'll be right with you. Here's Laura—she'll get you a drink,' before turning to open the door again.

Briar was halfway down the stairs by the time the newcomer had shaken hands with her father and exchanged some remarks about the imminence of summer. He had a deep, incisive voice, and curiosity made her glance up from her concentration on the stair carpet. At the same time he must have become aware of her moving down the stairs, and lifted his head, gazing past Xavier's shoulder.

Briar paused for an instant, surprised by a searching scrutiny from eyes the colour of old pewter, or a dawn sea. And—in spite of the unequivocal masculine reaction she discerned in them—as hard as metal and cold as a winter morning.

He was somewhere in his early thirties, she judged, his thick, dark hair untouched by grey, but there was a world of experience in those eyes, and in the taut planes of his cheeks, the carved-from-granite mouth. Even his stance, on the surface casual, one hand thrust into the pocket of a suit expertly tailored to a frame more appropriate to an athlete than a businessman, gave the impression of an underlying tensile strength. Perhaps it was the way his feet in their polished black leather were planted slightly apart on the Persian pattern, and the knife-edge crease of his trousers failed to conceal the latent power in his long legs.

He was taller than her father, who was well-built and not a small man, and she wondered if he lifted weights. Under the impeccable suit his shoulders were broad, his stomach flat. He looked superbly fit while not bulging with overdeveloped muscles.

As Briar descended the remaining stairs, he returned her involuntary inspection with interest, and a faint, knowing smile fleetingly curved his mouth. She felt the fine hair on her nape prickle. Very sure of himself, this man. Sure of his effect on women, too.

'There you are!' her father said, smiling expansively as he turned to her. 'Kynan, let me introduce you to my daughter. Briar, this is Kynan Roth. I told you about him.' He directed a meaningful glance at her, and Briar noticed that the other man sent a quick, probing look at his host before he took her extended hand and closed strong fingers about it.

His hand was warm and he held hers firmly before releasing it.

'Come along in, Kynan,' her father said, laying a hand on his guest's shoulder. Briar thought the shoulder stiffened. He hung back, allowing her to precede him and her father into the lounge. It was a large room furnished with comfortable leather chairs and sofas, solid mahogany coffee-tables, and some good antique cabinets and occasional pieces. The bar in one corner had been carefully designed to blend into the décor.

'I'll leave Briar to look after you,' her father said, giving the other man's shoulder a pat, 'if you don't mind. Catch up with you later.'

'I'm delighted.' A gleam entered the cool eyes as Kynan Roth murmured the polite response.

He didn't look delighted, Briar thought. He looked like a wary predator, circling for the kill but with one ear pricked for trouble.

She said, 'What would you like to drink?'

'What are you going to have?'

'A Chardonnay.' She didn't usually drink anything more than dry ginger ale this early in the evening at her father's parties, but something about this man was making her tense, and a glass of wine might relax her.

'Then I'll have the same.'

Surprise made her hesitate. He looked like a straight whisky man, or vodka on the rocks at least.

He raised his brows a fraction. 'Anything wrong?'

Briar shook her head and smiled, more at her thoughts than at him.

He didn't smile back, but something flickered in his eyes, and those slightly satanic brows momentarily drew together.

'Briar!' Her stepmother, draped in designer blue silk, clutched at her arm. 'There you are!'

Briar saw Kynan Roth's mouth twitch at the corner, his glance flicking from Laura to her as he obviously remembered her father's identical greeting, though delivered quite differently. He was looking at Briar now rather curiously.

'Laura,' she said, forestalling any outpouring of the latest imagined crisis—wine that hadn't been uncorked in time, a guest who had just now casually mentioned being a vegetarian, a last-minute begging-off leaving the table numbers uneven?—'this is Kynan Roth.'

Laura, remembering her manners, flashed a distracted smile. 'How do you do, Mr . . . ?' Then the name obviously penetrated and the sky-blue eyes widened. 'Oh! Oh, Mr Roth! Oh, I'm very pleased to meet you.' She held out her hand, but almost as though she anticipated it might be bitten off. Her gaze now was fascinated in the way a mouse was supposed to be fascinated by a snake. As Kynan took her hand she looked about anxiously. 'My husband . . . he'll be wanting to . . .'

'He let me in,' Kynan told her, releasing her fingers.

'Oh. Oh, good!' She was still looking at him. 'You're not at all what I expected.'

'Really?' He still didn't smile, yet Briar had the distinct impression he was beginning to enjoy himself. 'Tell me what you expected.' He bent his head towards Laura.

Laura blushed, the colour rising under her ageless white skin to the roots of her beautifully coiffured blonde hair. She looked helplessly at Briar.

Briar put a reassuring arm about her waist. 'I don't suppose Mr Roth expects you to answer that,' she said, fixing a social smile to her face.

Mr Roth looked as though he might be about to dispute her supposition, but Briar didn't give him a chance. 'He might not hear what he'd like to,' she went on, braving the faint spark that rose in the strangely metallic eyes. 'I was just about to fetch him a drink.' She withdrew her arm from Laura and took Kynan's, steering him away. 'The bar's this way.' If he got his kicks from teasing defenceless women, at least she could rescue Laura from him.

When they had their wine, he turned to her, lifting his glass. 'The name's Kynan,' he said, 'Briar.'

Be nice to him, her father had instructed. She curved the corners of her mouth upward and raised her glass. Her eyes fleetingly met his before sipping her wine gave her an excuse to look away. There was a concentration in his stare that made her uneasy.

She half turned from him, watching the other guests. All were representative of solid, respectable firms who managed the city's wealth, the kind of people her father had cultivated ever since, as a young, shrewd accountant with a hard-won degree and none of the right connections, he had set out to forge for himself a place in the upper echelons of Auckland's business community.

'Is there anyone I need to introduce you to?' she asked. She wondered if this evening had been arranged specifically to impress Kynan Roth.

He cast a cursory glance about. 'I've met some of the men.'

One of the women, Briar knew, was a successful barrister, another a well-known artist. But they were here because their husbands had been invited to bring them. Xavier found it difficult to cope with women in business.

'Would you like to meet their wives?' she asked.

His look seemed vaguely speculative. 'Would you mind?' he asked, a thread of something like laughter in his voice.

'Introducing you? Not at all.' She turned to lead him away from the bar, wondering why she'd thought there was a hidden meaning in his innocuous question. Then it hit her. He'd thought she'd been cutting him out for herself when she steered him away from Laura, that she'd decided not to let another woman near him.

She nearly laughed aloud. Automatically, her head swivelled to look back at him as he followed her, and he came closer to her and said, 'What?'

'Nothing.' She shook her head, indignation overcoming the laughter. She'd like to take him down more than a peg, but wrecking her father's dinner party wasn't the way to do it. Especially as Laura would field the blame.

She gave him a brilliant smile to hide her thoughts and led him towards a plump, pleasant-faced woman sitting on one of the deep leather sofas and twiddling with her glass while her husband talked with another man. Briar introduced them all to Kynan and, when he'd seated himself beside the woman with every appearance of pleasure, gracefully withdrew to find Laura and fix if necessary whatever was bothering her.

Apparently the crisis was over. Her father and stepmother were talking with another couple now. When she joined them, asking quietly, 'Is there something you wanted me to do, Laura?' she received a grateful smile and a whispered,

'It's all right, I think. The caterers said they'd sort it out.'

'I'm sure they will.' Briar smiled at the other couple and asked after their children, two at university and one still attending school.

As soon as their various whereabouts and latest exam results had been verified, Xavier broke into the conversation. 'Are you looking after Kynan, Briar?'

Suppressing a retort that she'd never met anyone less in need of looking after, Briar said patiently, 'I got him a drink and he's talking to Kath Bailey.'

Xavier frowned. 'You should have stayed with him.' Following his eyes, Briar saw Kath talking animatedly, her companion apparently listening with absorbed attention. Kath was a teacher, and, although she probably didn't have a lot in common with Kynan Roth, she wouldn't wilt with embarrassment if he should decide to have a little fun at her expense. In fact she'd probably give as good as she got, in the nicest way possible.

'He looks quite happy,' she pointed out.

Xavier said, 'Mmm. Well...I'll just.... Excuse me a moment.' And he nodded to the group and went over to the sofa.

Laura glanced at her watch. 'Dinner should be ready soon.' She took half a step towards the door, then stopped, apparently remembering her duty as hostess. 'Briar, would you...?'

'I'll check.' Briar was glad to leave the room. Laura seemed even more nervous than usual, and her father was like a cat on hot bricks. What could possibly be so significant about Kynan Roth?

She got no enlightenment over the meal, although he was seated next to her at the table. The dinner-party chat touched on the news of the day, skated over politics, and moved on to an exchange of views on best-selling books and the latest films, interspersed with business gossip.

Her father seemed surprisingly ready to concur with Kynan Roth's views—not that the younger man expressed them except when someone directly asked what he thought. And Laura, with her carefully rehearsed list of questions-to-keep-the-conversation-from-flagging, wasn't the only one who asked. The others seemed to find his opinion worth their attention, even if they disagreed. But most of the time he just listened, with an expression that Briar found impossible to define. Not boredom, exactly. More as though he was patiently waiting for some small glitter of gold to turn up in a pan of dross.

He seemed to have a good mind, and Briar respected that. He didn't dither about sitting on metaphorical fences, but considered other views and asked intelligent questions, seemingly in pursuit of information, not to score off an opponent. The perfect dinner guest, in fact.

Once he turned to her when a lively debate was going on among their neighbours, and said, 'Are you always so quiet?'

Briar put down her fork among the remnants of the artichoke on her plate and picked up her wine glass. 'When there's no particular need to talk,' she replied.

'What do you think of the government's moves on taxation, then?' he asked her.

It wasn't a question her father would ever have thought of asking a woman. She glanced up at Kynan, wondering if he expected her to disclaim any interest in or knowledge of the subject. Was he looking for an opportunity to indulge what she suspected was a heartless sense of humour?

His eyes held nothing that she could detect except a courteous curiosity.

Well, if he really wanted to know, she would tell him. She did, succinctly and logically. If he was surprised, he didn't show it. He raised a point or two that they tossed about between them while the caterers served succulent lamb garnished with paper-thin orange slices and mint sprigs, and then he slanted her an odd little smile before turning to answer a remark addressed to him from across the table.

When she refused dessert, he gave her another smile, accompanied by a quick, surmising and slightly humorous glance over her slim but well-defined figure. Then he spooned into a fluffy four-inch-high cheesecake topped with kiwifruit and strawberries on a thick layer of fresh whipped cream.

Briar was accustomed to people assuming that she skipped sweets because she was dieting, and usually it didn't bother her. Now, although he hadn't commented, she found herself biting her tongue to stop herself snapping, 'I just don't have a sweet tooth!' to correct Kynan Roth's tacit preconception.

When they all returned to the other room for coffee, she helped Laura pass the cups. Her father was talking to Kynan, who listened with his head inclined, his eyes intent and watchful. She let Laura take them coffee, carrying a second tray in the opposite direction. But when Kynan Roth's cup was empty, Xavier brought it to her for refilling, and muttered, 'Take this to Kynan, will you? There's an empty seat beside him now.'

She had to sit by him, since every other chair was occupied. He took his cup from her and regarded her over it before his eyes lowered and he took a sip. 'Good coffee,' he said. 'Where do you get it?'

'I've no idea. That's Laura's decision.' Laura was actually quite good at housekeeping and at backstage organisation, never leaving anything to chance because she suffered such agonies if the smallest thing went wrong. Her indecisiveness and nervous anxiety could drive people like her husband wild, but the professionals she employed liked her, perhaps because she was always grateful for their expert advice.

'You call your mother Laura?'

'Stepmother,' Briar explained briefly.

He didn't ask for details. 'You seem to get on well with her.'

'She's been extremely good to me.'

'A change from the stereotype.'

'Stereotypes are often wrong. I'm no Cinderella.'

'I can see that.' His gaze held a shade of mockery. 'And no ugly stepsisters?'

'No sisters or brothers of any sort.'

'You're an only child?'

'Yes.' Laura would have liked children of her own, she was sure. Briar didn't know if the lack of them had been an accident of fate or a deliberate choice of her father's.

A bearded man with an incipient paunch came over and said to Kynan, 'Kath tells me you're a cricketer.'

'Used to be,' Kynan answered. 'Nowadays I just watch, mostly.'

Clive Bailey, patting his expanding waistline, grinned. 'Me, too. Our son's a great little goer, though. Got any kids in the game, yourself?'

'No kids,' Kynan said easily. 'I'm not married.'

'Thing is,' Clive explained, 'our club's looking for coaches for the juniors——'

Briar finished her coffee and said, 'Please excuse me. I think Laura needs some help.'

Laura, as always preferring making herself busy to making conversation, had begun collecting empty cups. Kynan emptied his and handed it to Briar as she stood up. She gave him an automatic smile and went to join her stepmother. She'd done her duty by the special guest; her father ought to be satisfied that he'd not been neglected.

But later Xavier cornered her, with Kynan in tow beside him. 'Kynan's interested in early New Zealand paintings,' he told her with an air of something approaching triumph. 'I told him you'd show him our Heaphy in the library. I don't like to leave the other guests.'

The other guests, Briar might have told him, would almost certainly not be aware of his absence for five or ten minutes. Good manners prevailed. She mustered a pleasant smile and said, 'Of course.'

Xavier squeezed the other man's arm. 'Briar will look after you.'

Briar reflected that her father appeared to have decided that her mission in life was to look after Kynan Roth. She took a fleeting look at the object of all this attention, and found an ironic glint in his dark eyes, coupled with something else even more disturbing. It occurred to her that she didn't want to be alone with this man.

But she could hardly come to any harm in a room only two doors away from here. 'This way,' she said, turning as they reached the passageway.

He walked at her side, and when she reached out to open the library door he stepped quickly in front of her, so that she steeled herself not to snatch back her hand as his fingers closed about the gleaming brass knob. He cast her a questioning glance and swung open the door, then stood back to let her go first.

Xavier seldom read anything other than newspapers, financial magazines and business guides, though occasionally he skimmed through a book that had hit the best-seller lists or that someone had given him. But the previous owners had stocked the library with classics, travel books and biographies, to which had been added some well-reviewed modern fiction. Xavier frequently worked there on his portable computer, or waded through mountains of paperwork at the huge antique desk.

The Charles Heaphy original, a watercolour of a bracken-covered hillside washed in light, with a painstaking rendering of delicate ponga ferns in the foreground, hung on the wall to one side of the desk.

'That's it,' Briar said unnecessarily. Kynan was already crossing the carpet to inspect it.

Briar stood in the centre of the room waiting for him. Finally he said over his shoulder, 'Quite a good example, isn't it?' He returned his attention to the painting.

'Is it? I'm no expert, I'm afraid. I've always rather liked it, though.' She walked over to stand beside him, admiring it.

'Has it been in the family for long?' He glanced at her again.

'In the family?' She shook her head. 'Dad bought it a few years ago, when the financial wizards were saying that art was a gilt-edged investment for the future. I gather that it hasn't increased in value as much as he was led to believe it might.'

'So he's not a connoisseur?'

She wondered if her father had been trying to impress Kynan with art talk. Xavier was good at picking up snippets of information and trotting them out at opportune moments, giving the impression of more knowledge than he really had.

'Are *you*?' she countered, deflecting the question.

'I have an interest, but I doubt if I could spot a fake.'

'This isn't a fake.' Her father would have had that thoroughly checked.

He turned to her. 'I haven't suggested that it is. Not my field, except in an amateur way.'

'What is your field?' she asked him. She'd been wondering all evening. His name had sounded vaguely familiar, but she was unable to make the necessary connection.

'Didn't your father brief you?'

'Brief me?' She looked at him blankly, finding knowing laughter lurking in his eyes, and dropped her gaze as she recalled being told to be nice to him. She felt as though he was reading her mind, an uncomfortable sensation.

'I'm in company finance,' he told her, 'among other things.'

'An entrepreneur?'

'I prefer the term investor. These days entrepreneur tends to be a term of opprobrium.'

'How times have changed.'

'Are you old enough to remember?'

'I'm not a child.'

'No.' His eyes gleamed.

Briar looked away.

He said softly, 'You're not pretending to be shy?'

She looked up then, and found the cool, piercing eyes on her face, a hint of cynicism in them. 'I'm not shy.'

'No, I didn't think so. Your father tells me he depends on you a lot. I gather your stepmother isn't nearly as reliable.'

'She just needs a bit of self-confidence. She's...'

'Decorative?' Kynan suggested drily.

'She's also a very nice person!'

'I'm sure she is. How long have she and your father been married?'

'About thirteen years.'

'That long? You must have been just a kid.'

'A teenager—nearly. Laura was my salvation.'

'Oh?' His head cocked as though he wanted to hear more.

She wasn't prepared to exchange confidences with this discomfiting stranger. She opened her mouth to ask if he was ready to leave now, but he forestalled her. 'And are you prepared to be hers?' he asked. 'Or your father's?'

Feeling as though some piece of the conversation was missing, Briar said hesitantly, 'I...help when I can.'

'I'm sure you do.' He gazed at her almost broodingly. 'I suppose you all have a lot to lose.'

'I'm not sure what you mean.'

'All this——' he looked about them '—is very impressive. Gives the effect of a solid background.'

Her eyes sparked. 'Everything my father has he's got by his own efforts. He's never pretended to be anything he isn't.'

'Maybe that's a matter of opinion.'

Apprehension fluttered in her stomach. Something was wrong, and the supreme confidence of this man, contrasting with her father's peculiar nervousness tonight, had a lot to do with it.

He said, 'I only needed to ask around the financial community when he began pursuing my acquaintanceship, to find out why.'

With a trace of acid that brought a brief surprise to his eyes, Briar said, 'You mean it wasn't for the charm of your personality? And what did you find out?'

'That your father needs cash, and he needs it fast.'

Several things fell into place. Her anger dissolved in fright, which automatically she tried to conceal. 'I...don't know anything about my father's financial affairs,' she said. 'And if I did I wouldn't be discussing them with you.'

'No,' he said slowly, 'I suppose that isn't your role.'

Role? Whatever he meant by that, the expression on his face warned her that it wasn't good. He looked hard and contemptuous, and she didn't like the way he was studying her, his gaze moving from her defiant eyes down to her feet and slowly back again.

Stiffening under the visual assault, she said, 'I'm afraid I'm not up with the play. I've no idea what you're talking about.'

'Oh, come on.' He was smiling, in an oddly angry way. 'You've played it perfectly so far. Done everything darling Daddy told you to.'

He knew? 'My father is just being a good host,' Briar said. Some dim understanding of what he meant began to filter through her puzzlement. Her voice turned icy. 'This is your first time in our home and he hoped you'd enjoy the evening. I think you misunderstood. If you've finished in here...'

'Surely you're not finished yet? You don't need to give up on providing me with enjoyment just because I find you—and your father—a little...obvious.'

Briar took a deep, disbelieving breath. 'If this is some kind of game——'

'Isn't it?' he queried, his brows rising diabolically. 'I thought it was the oldest game in the world. Or should I say...profession?'

CHAPTER TWO

BRIAR felt almost dizzy. Anger brought a flush to her cheeks and buzzed in her head. She wanted to hit him, lash out with her hands, wipe the cool, scornful smile from his handsome face.

She clenched her fists at her sides, but her voice, a notch higher than usual, shook. 'I don't know how you usually conduct your business, Mr Roth, but I assure you that my father would never expect me to lower myself to that level. I suggest you get your mind out of the gutter! Or better still, crawl back in there where you belong. Excuse me, I need some clean air.'

She turned, making for the door, but was brought up short by a hard hand on her wrist pulling her about to face him.

Tugging at it, she said, eyes blazing, 'Don't you touch me!'

'Hang on there.' He easily swung her to one side, reaching over to push the door shut.

Alarmed, she tried to kick out at him, but he evaded it and let her go so suddenly that she almost lost her balance.

Now he was standing against the door, leaning on the panels with his hands in his pockets and his burnished-pewter eyes alert and bright.

'If you don't get away from that door I'll scream,' she threatened.

'Don't be silly, I'm not hurting you. Not even touching you, in fact.'

Her head went up, her mouth stubbornly set. 'I want to leave.'

'In a minute.' He was regarding her with speculation. 'Are you mad because I called your bluff, or because I was wrong in my assumptions?'

Briar's hand clenched. 'I'm not going to defend myself to you. You probably wouldn't believe me, anyway.'

'Try me,' he offered.

She debated trying to shove him aside, but although she was no weakling, he had the edge over her in both size and strength. She'd felt the power in his grip as he held her. 'You were wrong,' she said, her voice very even although she was sizzling inside. 'Totally, completely *wrong*.'

He seemed to be weighing that up, still steadily watching her. 'Your father didn't tell you to give me a good time?'

Briar felt her cheeks burn again. 'He didn't mean what you think.'

Softly, Kynan asked, 'Are you sure?'

An insidious doubt crept into her mind. Shaking it off, she said, 'Of course I'm sure. He wouldn't...and anyway, I wouldn't...'

Something like a grin briefly appeared on the chiselled mouth. 'I'm beginning to believe that you wouldn't.' He paused. 'I apologise.'

An apology was certainly due. 'Am I supposed to thank you for that?' she enquired.

The grin widened slightly. 'Not necessarily.'

'Good.' She was still simmering. 'Might I suggest you refrain from jumping to bizarre conclusions next time someone offers you their normal hospitality?'

'Oh, come on, Briar.' He folded his arms and crossed one ankle over the other, looking at her. 'What was I supposed to think? Your father was throwing you at me at every turn, and you certainly didn't seem to be objecting. You brought me in here on the flimsiest excuse——'

'He told me to——'

Kynan nodded. 'Are you always such a dutiful daughter? You seemed to be quite pleased with the idea.'

'I'm a good actress.'

He smiled openly at her tart tone. It made him look considerably less formidable. 'A natural,' he agreed. 'So...you don't really like me at all?'

'Should I?'

'Ouch!' he murmured. 'What should I do? Go down on my knees?'

She could hardly imagine it. 'You could start by moving away from the door.'

For a second or two he stayed there, then he unfolded his arms and stood aside, waiting.

Briar took an uncertain step forward, and Kynan leaned over and turned the handle, throwing the door wide.

'Thank you,' she said, sweeping past him into the passageway.

He closed the door and came to her side, saying nothing as they returned to the other room.

Some people were leaving, and Kynan took her arm in a light hold, drawing her closer to him to make way for them. Her father and Laura were seeing them out, Xavier casting Briar and Kynan a sharp glance.

'I should be going, too,' Kynan murmured. 'I think I may have outstayed my welcome.'

She gave him a sarcastic look, and he laughed. 'I'll go home and find some sackcloth and ashes,' he promised. 'Can you bear to say goodnight to me civilly?'

Briar regarded him stony-faced. It seemed to her he was taking the whole thing rather casually. He was doubtless used to charming birds from trees when he took a mind to it, but it would take more than a smile and a careless apology to mollify her. 'Goodnight,' she said, and held out her hand.

He looked down at it, smiling faintly, before he took it in his. 'Goodnight, Briar.' He turned her hand over, and raised her fingers fleetingly to his lips. She felt the warm brush of his mouth against her skin, and some unidentifiable sensation passed through her body. Then he released her and went to say goodnight to her father and stepmother.

Next day two huge florist's bouquets arrived at the house. One was addressed to Laura, with a card thanking her for dinner and an enjoyable evening, signed *Kynan Roth*. The other was for Briar.

She opened the envelope and read the card. There was nothing on it but his name. She supposed it was a reinforcement of his apology.

'Aren't they lovely?' Laura breathed in the scent of pink roses and carnations as she arranged them in a white porcelain vase. 'That's a man with style!' She looked sidelong at Briar. 'Did you . . . get along with him?'

'Does it matter?' Briar asked, tucking the card back into its envelope. Her bouquet featured yellow irises and deep creamy roses shading to gold in the centre. She wondered if he'd chosen the flowers himself.

'Oh, no! Not specially. Your father seemed to think...' Laura pushed a tall carnation into the vase, and the stem snapped in two. 'Oh, I'm so clumsy!'

'You're not. It was too long,' Briar pointed out absently. 'What's going on, Laura? Has Dad told you?'

'He doesn't tell me about his business affairs, you know that. But something has been bothering him.' Laura twiddled with the broken stem she had pulled from the vase, then dropped it and picked up the piece with the flower on it, regarding the arrangement uncertainly.

'What did he say?'

'Nothing much at all,' Laura said quickly. 'But I know he's worried.'

'Financial problems?' Kynan Roth had said so, but why should she believe him? Her father had always been successful. Some years ago he had moved from straight accountancy to setting up a financial advice and investment service. He was regarded as a man who knew where the best deals were to be made. Lawyers and accountants often referred to him clients who had some money set aside and were unsure as to where to invest it.

'I suppose so,' Laura said. 'When I asked him what was the matter he said there's been a downturn in the share-market, but he's sure things will straighten themselves out.'

'Is he hoping to attract some investment money from Kynan Roth?'

'I don't know. He said more than once that he couldn't afford to lose Mr Roth, so I was to make sure he enjoyed himself and that there were no slip-ups last night. But knowing how important it was just made me go to pieces.'

'You did fine.'

'Do you think so? I must admit that Mr Roth was perfectly nice, although something about the man makes me nervous. It was kind of him to send flowers. Didn't you like him?'

'Not specially,' Briar answered crisply. 'Did Dad say that he wanted me to...?'

'What?' Laura turned enquiring blue eyes on her.

'Never mind, it wasn't important.' Laura was inclined to make a big worry out of quite trivial things. She might have blown up a casual remark out of proportion to its real significance, Briar told herself. It wouldn't be the first time.

Of course her father hadn't set her up with Kynan. Not deliberately. He might have had some vague hope that if they took to each other it would make a business arrangement easier to bring about. He certainly hadn't been asking her to sell herself in return for some of Kynan's money.

Over lunch, Xavier asked her, 'How did you get on with Kynan Roth?'

She looked up from her salad. 'All right.' And bluntly she asked, 'Why?'

'No particular reason. I thought you might enjoy meeting someone nearer your age...'

'I meet people my age all the time,' Briar said. 'Who exactly is Kynan Roth, anyway?'

'He's been overseas for a number of years—he was chief executive of a big Australian steel firm. When his father died last year he came home to take over the family company. Created quite a stir. Bit of a whiz-kid.'

'Quite a number of whiz-kids lost their shirts in the last crash, didn't they?' Briar commented.

'Yes, indeed. Got caught on the market with their pants down. Young idiots who flew around in their corporate jets taking over companies and throwing champagne parties every time their shares doubled in value.' Xavier's lips curled distastefully. 'Roth's not that sort.

The business has a rock-solid base, manufacturing plants that have been in the family for a long time. He brought new ideas back with him and expanded the original company. Old money and business acumen are a winning combination.'

'Big money?'

'Hundreds of millions. Low profile, like his father, but it's there, all right.'

'He said you need cash.'

Xavier looked at her sharply. 'When did he say that?'

'Last night, when I was showing him the Heaphy. Is that why you asked me to be nice to him?'

A dull flush rose in Xavier's neck. 'He's a useful contact, just like all the others who were here last night.'

'As a possible source of quick money?'

Laura put down her fork. 'Do you want some more ham, Briar?'

'This is business, Briar,' her father said dismissively. 'You wouldn't understand.'

Briar's glance at her stepmother was apologetic, but she turned again to her father. 'Just how important to you is this man?'

Xavier replied testily, 'Nothing to worry about. I simply need a bit of short-term finance to cover a temporary cash-flow problem.'

Alarm bells were ringing in Briar's head. 'You're hoping he'll give you a loan?'

'A business loan is more complicated than—than mortgaging a house, or buying a car on hire-purchase.'

Laura's smooth brow creased. 'You won't have to mortgage the house, will you?'

'The house! It wouldn't begin to cover——' Xavier scowled. 'Wherever did you get that idea?'

'I suppose,' Briar said, 'you could sell the Heaphy.'

'A few thousand dollars!' Xavier gave a rather harsh laugh. 'It won't come to that. I told you, it's nothing to worry about.'

He bent his attention to the cold mutton on his plate. Briar's eyes met Laura's over the table. Laura's blue gaze was clouded, and the frown had not left her face.

The phone rang as the two women were stacking the dishwasher after lunch, and Laura went to answer it. Hearing her muted voice in the hall, Briar assumed the call was for her stepmother. But after a minute or two Laura called, 'Briar—can you come to the phone?'

As Briar took the receiver, Laura whispered, 'It's Kynan Roth!' She retreated back to the kitchen as Briar lifted the receiver to her ear.

'Thank you for the flowers,' Briar said formally. 'They're beautiful.'

'I'm glad you like them. Have you forgiven me, yet?'

She deliberately let half a second elapse before she said coolly, 'Of course.'

Faint laughter came down the line. 'But not entirely? Let me make amends——'

'I thought that was what the flowers were for.'

'They haven't done the trick, have they? I'd like to take you to dinner tonight, if you're free.'

'On the theory that an evening in your company will "do the trick"?' she enquired drily.

'Nasty, Briar! On the theory that a good dinner in a comfortable restaurant might have a soothing effect. Where would you like to go?'

'With you? I'm not sure that I want to go anywhere.'

Laura appeared in the kitchen doorway, a plate in her hand, her expression tense. She'd been listening, Briar realised. As her eyes met Briar's, she gave an apologetic smile and ducked back.

'But you are free tonight?' Kynan was asking.

As she debated over whether to admit she was, he said, 'Have you been to Benedict's?'

'Not yet.' It was a new place that had opened in a blaze of publicity. The owners were said to have lured the best chef in town from his previous position in the kitchen of a top hotel.

'I'll book us a table,' he said. 'Pick you up at seven, OK?'

She wanted to tell him no, it wasn't OK at all. But Laura's disquiet had communicated itself to her. She hesitated and was lost.

'See you then,' Kynan said. And she was left holding the phone, with the dialling tone humming in her ear.

She wore an apricot wild silk jacket over a flowered skirt and soft jade green blouse, and put on the highest heels in her wardrobe, remembering that Kynan Roth was a tall man. She didn't want him towering over her.

He arrived promptly and she opened the door to him herself. Laura had already served a meal for herself and Xavier, and they were watching a favourite programme in the TV room. 'Briar's going out with Kynan Roth,' Laura had told Xavier brightly.

Watching her father's face, Briar thought he seemed almost disconcerted. Then he'd said, a shade too loudly, 'Well, that's nice, Briar. Must have taken a fancy to you.'

Kynan ushered her into the passenger seat of a shiny dark blue car. He had manners, if nothing else, she reflected. And quickly amended that—as well as everything else. Money, good looks, power, and the sex appeal that went with them. All the superficial advantages were his.

And superficial they were, she reminded herself as he slid into the driver's seat, smiling at her before starting the engine. There were more important qualities that she looked for in a man. Compassion, kindness, understanding, the capacity to love, and a sense of humour.

He had that last, but she wasn't sure if there was any warmth or gentleness behind it. An ability to laugh at others didn't necessarily go with an equal willingness to laugh at oneself.

She concentrated on the view from the side-window—the big, rambling old houses and professional buildings lining Remuera Road. But as Kynan stopped for a red light she peeped speculatively at his profile, eyeing the jutting nose and strong chin.

He turned as though he'd felt her gaze, and asked, 'What's that for?'

'What?' She looked away, watching a woman walk by on the pavement with a Siamese cat on a leash.

'That look you just gave me,' he said.

'I was wondering if you can laugh at yourself.' She raised her chin and met his eyes.

'Think I can't?' He stared back at her.

Behind them a horn tooted gently. 'The light's changed,' she told him.

He gave the other driver a wave, and sent the car gliding over the intersection. Picking up speed, he kept his eyes on the road and the traffic. 'You didn't seem to think I was particularly funny,' he said, 'last night.'

Last night she'd thought he was particularly insulting. 'I wasn't thinking of last night. Just...in general.'

'Well...' He slanted her a glance. 'Perhaps you'll find out, in time.'

Which suggested that they'd be seeing each other again after tonight.

They cruised through the Newmarket shopping area, and then crested a hill and drove past the colonial-style shops and trendy eating places in Parnell village. He didn't speak again until they reached the restaurant down near the harbour, and he let her out of the car.

Briar half expected him to take over ordering her meal for her. Instead he allowed her to make her own choice and consulted her preference before deciding on the wine. The restaurant was crowded, but their table, lit by a single candle and discreetly dim wall-lighting, was screened by a couple of plants and a trellised partition, and next to a window overlooking a glimpse of the Waitemata Harbour. She wondered if he'd asked for it specially. 'Have you been here before?' she asked him.

'Once. The food's good. And the service.'

'And the view.' The darkened water reflected the lights of the city near the shore. Further out the moonlight had washed it with a subtle silvery patina. 'It's lovely.'

'Mm-hmm.' But when she looked back, his eyes were on her face. 'You're looking wonderful tonight,' he said. 'I've been telling myself all day you couldn't be as beautiful as I remembered.'

'I...thank you.' She wasn't unaccustomed to compliments. She'd travelled in Italy and France, and the men there weren't backward in their comments on a woman's appearance. But she was oddly flustered now. He didn't sound admiring, but rather as if he was reporting a fact, almost clinically detached.

He said, 'I've never seen eyes that colour before. Like moonlight on water.'

Instinctively she glanced out at the moonlit harbour, and returned her gaze to his in frank disbelief.

Kynan looked briefly out at the view, too. 'Not quite the same, I admit. They remind me of nightfall in the Islands.'

Briar gave a little laugh.

'What's funny?'

'My eyeshadow,' she said, 'is called "Tropic Dusk".'

'It's a perfect description.' He leaned over and brushed a finger very lightly over her eyelid. 'I didn't realise you were wearing shadow.' He looked at the faint smudge on his finger and his eyes gleamed as he raised them again to hers.

She studied the starched white tablecloth, fiddled with a polished silver fork, and lifted a hand nervously to brush a strand of hair from her cheek.

'Tell me about yourself,' he invited.

'What, everything?' She looked up. She wasn't shy or nervous, normally. He was only a man, and she'd had dealings with equally sophisticated men before, just as handsome, just as sure of themselves. Well, almost.

'Where did you go to school?' he asked. 'Diocesan?'

Briar grimaced. 'How did you guess?'

He laughed. 'It isn't hard, is it?'

Given what he knew or had guessed of her background, Briar had to admit it wasn't. Xavier had always gone for the best. The most socially acceptable.

'And after that—what?' he asked, and answered for her, 'University, right?'

'Right,' Briar conceded.

'And a Bachelor of Arts degree, which you got easily.'

'Am I that predictable?'

'And then...you did your Overseas Experience. Along with a couple of girlfriends. Or a boyfriend.'

'I went with a group of both sexes.'

'Anyone special, for you?'

'We made a pact before we left. No pairings. We had a great time, without hassles or emotional tangles.'

'Where did you go?'

This was safe ground. She talked about her travels until their food arrived, and then asked if he'd done much travelling himself.

'Closer to home, mostly. I crewed on a schooner round the Pacific Islands when I was younger.'

That was interesting, and she plied him with questions while they finished their dinner. And discovered that he did have an ability to laugh at himself—at least at his younger self, fighting seasickness in a mid-ocean squall, being the butt of a practical joke involving a fake shark fin in a lagoon in the Cook Islands, falling from a coconut palm when he tried to emulate the Fijians who climbed to the top with deceptive ease.

'Were you hurt?' she asked him.

'Fortunately the sand was soft. I bruised my ego, that's all. And took some teasing about it afterwards.' He pushed his plate aside. 'You don't eat sweets, do you?'

'Sometimes. I'd prefer cheese tonight, but don't let me stop you.'

He shook his head. 'I'll join you. A cheese board,' he said to the waiter who had appeared to take their plates. 'And then coffee?' He looked at Briar enquiringly.

'Yes, thank you.'

Cutting herself a wedge of pale, delicately flavoured havarti, she asked, 'So how do you become an investor? My father said you'd inherited a manufacturing company.'

He was placing a slice of gruyère on a cracker. When he looked up she thought he seemed wary. 'My father's firm made parts for ship-building. When he took over it already had a healthy profile. He expanded the base, used the profits to buy up various companies in related fields. His business judgement was impeccable.' A bitter expression crossed his face, so fleetingly that Briar decided she'd imagined it.

'And the firm survived when others went bust.'

'He'd never over-extended on the basis of cash that he didn't have. Since I took over I've tried to invest as wisely. And I've had a certain amount of luck.'

'Luck?'

'There's an element of risk involved,' he said. 'What I like to do is step in when a firm is shaky but basically viable, save a good business from going down the drain, taking investors and staff with it. One of my purchases turned out to be a dud but the others covered the loss. Our shares haven't made huge overnight gains. On the other hand, they're steady climbers. They're worth more than twice what they were a few years back.'

'You're a bit of a gambler?'

He picked up the cheese knife, then put it down again. 'Is this leading somewhere?'

'What do you mean?' As his brows went up in scepticism, she felt a flush rise to her cheeks. 'You asked me to tell you about myself. I was simply returning the compliment.' She was angry, and didn't care if he knew it.

After a moment he said, 'OK.' And he reached over and touched her hand, just a light touch on her skin. Oddly, she felt a tiny fluttering in her stomach, almost as though he'd threatened her in some way.

The coffee came, and she was glad of the diversion. She spooned cream into hers and stirred it broodingly.

'So what do you do all day?' he asked her.

'I help out in a boutique in Newmarket owned by a friend. Fashion accessories.'

He didn't seem madly impressed. She supposed it was small beer compared with his business empire. 'I see,' he said. 'How long have you been doing that?'

'About a year. Before that I worked for a market research firm, but they laid off some staff and it was last in, first out. And I've been a kennelmaid, receptionist, theatre assistant—before the theatre company went bust. Of course, overseas I picked up odd jobs—fruitpicking, waitressing—once I worked as a nanny for a little while.'

'A pretty varied working life,' Kynan commented.

'I like variety. I was never blessed—or cursed—with a burning ambition for a particular career.' She was happy to have work of any sort that provided her with some independence.

'And you still live at home?'

'Since I came back from overseas.' His tone was noncommittal, but she found herself reacting defensively. 'It's convenient and Laura likes having me there.' When she had first returned she'd intended to go flatting. But Laura had seemed so relieved to have her home, and her father had taken it for granted that she'd stay. Somehow she had never made the move.

'There's no man in your life?'

'If there was,' she said, 'I wouldn't be here with you.'

'You're the faithful type?' he mocked, as though he didn't believe that such a type existed.

'If I loved a man,' she said, 'I'd be faithful to him.'

'And have you?'

'Have I...?'

'Ever loved a man?'

'I'm not sure I...know what you mean.'

His mouth quirked. 'It's a simple question, but you don't have to answer if you don't want to.'

It wasn't a simple question at all. Of course she'd been in love, briefly and blindingly—and falsely, as it turned out. Because that couldn't be real love, that died so easily and so fast. Real love, lasting love, was a different thing altogether. It hadn't happened to her yet, and maybe never would. She only hoped that when it did she would recognise it. But what he'd been asking—what she'd thought he was asking—was if she'd had a lover in the physical sense.

'It's a very personal question,' she said.

'I'll withdraw it if you like,' he offered easily, as though it didn't matter, after all. 'Maybe... one day I'll find out the answer.'

His smile glinted. Briar drew in a breath, ready to slay him with words, but of course that was what he was waiting for, her rising to the bait. And then he'd go all innocent and deny that he'd meant what she thought. She knew that game.

Well, she wasn't going to play it with him. She kept her expression blank and raised her coffee-cup to her lips. Putting it down again, she said pleasantly, 'That was a wonderful meal. Thank you.'

Kynan inclined his head. 'Not at all. It was worth it for the pleasure of your company.' He finished his coffee and asked, 'More for you?'

Briar shook her head.

He paid the bill and took her arm as they left the restaurant. 'It's a nice night,' he said. 'Feel like a stroll along the waterfront?' The scent of the sea came faintly to them. Moonlight still shimmered on the horizon.

It wasn't late. Cars constantly passed by under the green glow of the street-lights. The night air was cool but pleasant. 'All right,' she heard herself say. 'A short one.'

They walked slowly, and he took her hand and tucked it into his arm. She might have withdrawn it except for the darkness which the street-lights didn't altogether dispel, and the high heels of her shoes. It wouldn't do to trip and fall at his feet.

After a while they stopped and leaned on a guard-rail, looking out at the water and the multicoloured reflected lights, ceaselessly moving, and breaking into disjointed lines. Small, unseen wavelets lapped at the shore, and a fishy, salty scent rose from the breakwater. Briar removed her hand from Kynan's and placed it on the cold metal of the railing.

Kynan turned and leaned back so that he could see her face. His elbows rested on the rail. 'What did your father say when you told him you were going out with me?' he asked her.

Briar glanced at him briefly. 'Nothing.'

'Nothing?'

'He said you must have taken a fancy to me.' She tilted her head, challengingly.

Kynan gave a breathy laugh. 'Not, "Good girl"?'

Briar drew away from the guard-rail, taking a step back from him. 'I thought you'd admitted you were wrong about that.'

'About you,' he corrected her. 'And your father is no fool. He's right, of course. I have taken a fancy to you— just as he wanted me to.' His voice was light, but there was an undercurrent to it that made her decidedly uncomfortable.

'Am I supposed to be flattered?'

'You needn't be.'

She wasn't at all sure what he was getting at. Why did she have the feeling that half of this conversation wasn't taking place between the two of them at all, but somewhere inside his head?

'I'm cold,' she said.

His teeth gleamed whitely for a second. 'Sure.' He sounded as though he didn't believe her for an instant. He knew she was retreating. 'I'll take you back to the car.'

He drove her home in silence, and she felt stifled and fidgety the whole time. At the house he got out and came round to her door, but she was already on the pavement when he reached her.

'Thank you,' she said. 'The meal was delicious.'

'You're not going to ask me in?'

'I need an early night. We had a party last night, remember.'

'Aren't you used to late nights?' He was looking at her curiously.

'I don't spend my life at parties, if that's what you mean.'

'How about tomorrow afternoon?'

'What about it?'

'It's Sunday,' he said patiently. 'Are you free in the afternoon? Do you like cricket?'

'You don't need to offer me any more outings,' she said. 'The dinner was more than adequate atonement.'

'Meaning, you don't want to see me again?'

Why was he insisting on making her spell it out? She lifted a shoulder, not saying anything.

His voice soft, he said, 'Playing hard to get, Briar?'

She almost choked on her indrawn breath. 'If you still think that my father——'

He made a small, derisive sound. 'This has nothing to do with your father. It's to do with you—and me.'

Bewildered, she demanded, 'What are you talking about?'

'This,' he said tersely, and he reached for her and pulled her into his arms and kissed her before she could do anything about it, driving her astonished lips apart with stunning eroticism. His mouth was warm and firm and compelling, and he gathered her body against his as if he knew that was where it belonged, with a sureness and grace that had her pliant as a willow branch for long seconds, before she stiffened and thrust her hands against him, wrenching herself away, her breath coming fast between her open, moistened lips.

He said, 'That's what I was talking about. If I took a fancy to you—and I did—at least it's mutual. So stop pretending, Briar. Let's be honest about it.'

CHAPTER THREE

BRIAR hadn't known. She felt stupid that she hadn't known it until then. He was right. And he'd recognised, long before she did, that the unsettling effect he had on her was due to basic sexual instinct that had seethed beneath the surface and manifested itself in the uncomfortable emotional reactions she'd mistaken for dislike and even fear.

She'd been right the first time she saw him when she'd thought he was far too knowing and too sure of himself. It was humiliating that he'd proved his point so easily, but at least now she knew about her own vulnerability and she'd not let him take her unawares again.

'Sex on its own,' she said, 'doesn't interest me.'

Kynan laughed. 'It doesn't interest me, either. Mutuality is much more satisfying.'

She was glad it was dark enough that the heat in her cheeks wouldn't be visible. 'I meant,' she said, fighting for some dignity, 'that I'm not in the market for a casual fling with any passing stranger.'

He cocked his head to one side. 'Are you so responsive to every passing stranger who happens along?'

'You know I'm not!' she snapped.

'How could I know? We only met——'

'That's just my point!'

'Ah. You feel we should know each other better before indulging in . . . intimacies.'

Briar found her fists were clenched. 'I've no intention of indulging in anything of the kind!'

41

'Not even when you know me better?'

'I don't *want* to know you better! I have no desire——'

His laughter interrupted her. 'Liar. Why don't you want to get to know me?'

'I have no desire,' she said deliberately, 'to get to know a self-satisfied, smug, egotistical——'

'I get the idea,' he interrupted. 'You don't like me.'

'No, I don't!'

He grinned. 'Do you always jump to conclusions about people you hardly know?'

'Only when their behaviour warrants it.'

He leaned forward a little, bringing his face closer to hers. 'But you liked kissing me, Briar,' he reminded her softly. 'You can't deny *that*.'

'That doesn't mean you had a right to do it!'

Changing tack abruptly, he said, 'I thought you were enjoying yourself, tonight. Or was that another demonstration of your acting ability? Don't bother to be polite,' he added with some irony.

Tempted to dispute it, she hesitated and reluctantly admitted, 'It was very...pleasant.'

'Damned with faint praise,' he murmured. 'And the kiss was pleasant too, wasn't it? A nice way of rounding off the evening, I thought.'

'No, you didn't. You meant to teach me a lesson.'

He was still for a moment, then he gave a slight shrug. 'Maybe that was a part of it. But mostly, I'd been wanting to kiss you ever since we met.' He paused. 'Don't tell me you weren't aware of it.'

She'd seen the attentive interest in his eyes in that first instant when he looked up and saw her coming down the stairs. She couldn't refute that. She looked away from him. 'If you mean that I should have expected to have to pay for my dinner——'

'*I'd stop there if I were you*!' His voice sent a small shiver of fright down her spine. She forced herself to meet his gaze again, defiance in her eyes, but she couldn't find any more words.

His eyes were very dark, and even in this light she could see the angry spark in them. 'Don't push me too far, Briar,' he warned.

'Are you threatening me?' She faced him, her chin squared.

He looked down at her and suddenly laughed again. 'No.' He lifted a hand and flicked at her cheek with his finger. 'I'm telling you to watch those thorns of yours, my sweet rose.'

She jerked her head away from the tiny stinging touch. 'I'm not yours, and I'm not *sweet*!'

He was smiling at her, enjoying this. 'I'd noticed. But I'm sure you could be if you put your mind to it. Think about it.' And he swung on his heel and went back round the car.

With his hand on the door-handle, he said, 'Go into the house.'

She was standing where he had left her, and she turned and walked quickly up the path, not looking round as she fumbled with the lock and let herself in. As she closed the door she heard the sound of his car moving away.

To her annoyance she did think about it—about him, anyway—quite a lot over the next few days. Trying to put him out of her mind simply didn't work. Her brain insisted on going over and over things he'd said, and her body kept reacting to memories of the way he'd held her and kissed her and woken that unexpected response.

Her father had wanted to know, over breakfast the following morning, how her evening had been.

'Very nice, thank you,' was all the reply she was prepared to give him.

But after a few minutes he'd said, as though unable to contain himself, 'Well, will you be seeing him again?'

'I don't think so.' Briar kept her voice casual.

'You didn't offend him, did you?'

'No.' She might have, she supposed, with her assessment of his character, but he'd shown no sign of being mortally wounded. If anything, he'd found it amusing. 'I thought you said he wasn't all that important. Why are you so anxious?'

'I'm not anxious,' her father asserted. 'But at your age you ought to be thinking about...things. It wouldn't do you any harm to encourage him.'

Laura said, 'But if Briar doesn't like him, Xavier——'

'What's wrong with him?' her husband demanded. 'Kynan Roth is a very good catch for a girl.'

Laura said, 'Briar is a very good catch, herself. Any man would be lucky to have her.'

'Thank you, Laura.' Briar smiled at her. 'But I'm not actually thinking of marriage—and neither, I'm sure, is Kynan. I doubt if he's the marrying kind.'

Laura said confidently, 'Every man is the marrying kind. They need it more than we do.'

Xavier bent a surprised stare on his wife. 'What gave you that idea?'

'I read it somewhere. Men marry more quickly after they lose a partner, and are happier when they're married. Women are happier single. Statistically speaking,' Laura added hastily, ducking her head.

'I don't believe it,' Xavier said bluntly.

Laura cast her stepdaughter a lightning-fast glance, then turned an innocent gaze to her husband. 'Well, that's what it said.'

'I'm certainly happy being single,' Briar declared.

'Are you saying you don't want to marry?' her father asked, a hint of outrage in his voice.

'Not yet. Maybe never. But if the right man came along...'

'How do you know Kynan Roth isn't the right man for you?'

'He does seem very eligible,' Laura murmured. 'Handsome, too. And thoughtful. Not many men will phone their hostess to thank her for a party, and even fewer send flowers...'

'Do you want to marry me off, too?' Briar asked her.

'No, of course not! I love having you here, I don't know what I'd do without you. But we don't want to selfishly keep you at home.'

'You're not a bit selfish. And you don't really need my help.'

Laura looked doubtful, and Xavier gave a snort that made his daughter throw him a quick glance, but he didn't seem to notice.

'Anyway,' Briar said, 'Kynan isn't likely to suggest seeing me again.'

He'd probably go off and find someone who was less prickly. And good luck to him.

So she was startled when one day she looked up from serving a customer in the boutique and saw an unmistakable dark head bent over a rack of silk scarves in a corner.

When she had wrapped the customer's purchase and the woman had left the shop, Kynan turned and smiled at her. 'So this is where you are,' he said.

Did that mean his visit was coincidence? She hadn't told him the name of the shop or exactly where it was. She said, safely, 'Yes. Can I help you?'

He surveyed her silently for a moment, as though debating what to say. Then he smiled again. 'Sure. I want to buy someone a present.'

'A woman?' There were racks of men's ties and unisex scarves, but he was in the section containing more obviously feminine wear, and she came out from behind the counter to stand on the other side of the circular display rack.

'Yes, a woman.'

'Do you know what colours she likes? What kind of clothes she feels comfortable in? Casual or dressy? And is she dark or fair or——?'

'Dark,' he said. 'Dark-haired, fair-skinned. Brown eyes. She reads *Vogue* and shops at Saks. Her favourite oufit is a sort of rusty red suit and a blouse with lots of green in it. And she's just bought herself a red dress.'

He knew a lot about her, Briar thought. She wondered how long he'd known this woman—and how intimately.

Not that it was any concern of hers, of course. As two more people entered the shop, she turned her attention to the scarves, pushing aside a couple of tie-dyed ones and another in blue and green stripes. 'Perhaps this?' she suggested, pulling out a big silk square printed with autumn leaves. 'Or this?' The pattern was abstract, a daring combination of green, orange and red splashed with black.

'Mmm,' he said, fingering the second one. 'I think she'd like that.' He took it from her and spread it between his hands, finally nodding. 'I'll take it.'

So 'she' was no conservative dresser, Briar deduced. 'Would you like it gift-wrapped? And I can give you a card, if you like.'

'Thank you.' He slid a hand into his breast pocket and took out a brown leather wallet. 'How much?'

He hadn't looked at the price tags. The scarf wasn't a cheap one, but he put down a fifty-dollar note on the counter without comment.

Another customer approached, holding two packets of tights. Cutting off a piece of gift-wrap, Briar called through the screened doorway leading to the back of the shop, 'Pat? Can you serve?'

She deftly wrapped the parcel and was showing Kynan a card for his approval when Pat came in and Kynan looked up, his gaze suddenly arrested.

'All right?' Briar prompted him.

He turned to her. 'Yes. That's fine.' His eyes went back to her partner. 'I hadn't realised——'

Puzzled, she glanced at the red-headed young man by her side who was serving the other customer. It dawned on her that Kynan had expected her friend and employer to be female.

He was looking at her again now, a peculiarly searching look. She smiled at him blandly and handed him the card. 'Do you want to write something in it?'

He scrawled, 'Love, Kynan' on the inside. She could read it, even upside-down and trying not to. He hadn't attempted to hide it. She placed the card in the parcel and made a professional job of wrapping it before tucking the fifty dollars in the till and handing him the change.

He picked up the parcel and stood as though weighing it in his hand. Then he said, 'What time do you finish here?'

'We lock up at five tonight, and spend about ten minutes cashing up.'

Pat glanced at her curiously as he reached across to the till, and she stepped back to give him room.

Kynan waited until the other transaction was finished, the two people had left, and Pat was moving away to help another customer who was picking up bags and belts at random and replacing them.

'Come and have a drink with me before you go home,' Kynan suggested. 'Or better still, let me take you to dinner.'

She couldn't help being pleased that he wanted to see her again, after all. Vanity, she told herself, pure and simple. He might not have sought her out today, but now he didn't want to leave without making sure of her company for an hour or two.

Involuntarily she looked down at the package he held, and he laughed. 'It's for my mother. Her birthday present.'

'I wasn't——'

'Of course not.' But his eyes said, *Of course you were wondering*. 'Can I call for you later?'

Why not? He was a trifle arrogant and inclined to take too much for granted, but he certainly hadn't bored her the night he'd taken her to dinner, and accepting a glass of wine or two wouldn't commit her to anything. She had nothing else in particular to do tonight. 'All right,' she said. 'Drinks. I'll meet you in front of the shop.'

* * *

'Do you bring a car to work?' he asked her when she joined him on the pavement among the workers hurrying home.

'Not usually. I take the bus, or walk if it's fine and I have the time.'

'Then we'll take my car and I'll drop you back at home afterwards.'

He took her to a restaurant that had a quiet bar with deep leather chairs flanking smoked-glass tables. When they'd almost finished their second round of drinks, he leaned back and gave her a gravely speculative look, asking, 'So—do I order a table for dinner?'

'If you like.' She looked down at the cocktail glass cradled in her hands. And then, thinking that she was being ungracious, she lifted her eyes to his. 'I'd enjoy that.'

He smiled at her. 'So would I.'

'I'll just use the phone and let Laura know I'm not coming home till later.'

Over dinner he said, 'I thought your friend who owned the boutique would be a woman.'

Her mouth curved in amusement. 'Yes, I know.'

His lips quirked, too. 'Did you mislead me on purpose?'

'No! It just...didn't come up. Pat and I knew each other at university. He used to go with a girlfriend of mine. That broke up, but we always got on well.'

'You're on wages?'

'Yes, of course. I don't work for him free.'

'I thought you might have put some capital in the business.'

She shook her head. 'I'm just a worker. I don't have any urge to own a business.'

'And you're still just friends?'

He sounded sceptical, and her look was faintly hostile. 'Why do you want to know?'

'Maybe I'm jealous,' he suggested, but not as though he meant it.

'You've no right to be jealous of me.'

'Granted. I'm not prone to it.'

Which meant he'd been teasing, she supposed. Although she knew very well there'd been an element of instinctive male rivalry in this invitation, issued right after he'd met Pat. 'I don't believe you, anyway.'

He laughed. 'It was kind of you to help me choose my mother's present.'

Briar looked at him suspiciously. 'It's part of the job,' she assured him, 'satisfying the customers.'

He lifted a brow at her, but refrained from making any comment.

He took her home quite early, and this time he didn't try to kiss her, just leaned over and opened the car door, but before she could get out he caught her wrist lightly and said, 'Shall we do this again?'

It had been an enjoyable evening. She wasn't sure why she remained wary of him, except that even now she had a feeling he was speaking against his own better judgement. 'Call me,' she said, not wanting to commit herself.

He tightened his hold as she made to move away, and said, 'I'd rather not.'

Briar turned her head in surprise, to find him momentarily staring through the windscreen in front of him. He looked round at her and said, 'If you don't mind, I'd prefer that your parents didn't know.'

'Why?'

'Let's say, I have my reasons. And it isn't because I've a wife and six children hidden away in the suburbs.' He paused. 'Clive Bailey inveigled me into coaching one of the teams in his son's cricket club. They have a game next Sunday at Orewa. Care to come and watch it with me?'

'And cheer on the team?'

'If you like. We could have a meal afterwards.'

'All right. It sounds like fun.'

She saw a new side of him that day. Surrounded by ten-year-olds, he was relaxed and tolerant, and they obviously adored him. Briar stood on the sidelines with him, clapping runs and catches, and commiserating when the team lost the game.

'Never mind,' he told the disconsolate junior cricketers. 'You played your best, and that's what counts. I'll see you all at practice on Wednesday, and maybe next time it'll be our turn to win. Now, who wants an ice-cream?'

'Me-e!' a chorus of young voices shouted, and Kynan laughed and handed over a couple of notes to the captain. 'OK, see that shop over there? But I want you all back here in ten minutes. Your bus driver will be waiting.' He'd driven out in his car with Briar while the youngsters shared a hired bus with another team and half a dozen parents.

Briar commented, 'You like children, don't you?'

'Haven't had a lot to do with them,' Kynan said, 'but I've enjoyed coaching the team. They're good kids. They can play up on occasion but they respond well to bribes and threats of physical violence.'

Briar laughed. 'Is that how you keep them in line?'

'Is there another way?' He smiled down at her, and she couldn't help responding to it with a slight increase in her pulse rate.

When the boys and their minders had left, Kynan and Briar went walking on the nearby beach, a long stretch of pale sand washed by shallow breakers spreading lazily over the shore in long, curved lines. Because of its proximity to the city, Orewa was a popular resort and retirement settlement, and houses and motels fronted the shoreline. But the beach was nearly deserted at this time of day, save for a couple of fishermen and an elderly couple strolling hand in hand.

Kynan took Briar's hand too, and she let him, liking the feel of his fingers laced into hers. She had taken off her shoes and left them in his car, and the sand was firm under their feet. Once or twice a wave came close enough to leave a cool kiss on her toes. A breeze ruffled her hair, and wound her full skirt about her legs. She felt Kynan's gaze on her, and looked up, to find him looking back at her with a frankly sexual stare.

Her gaze fell away, her fingers slackening in his, but he silently tightened his grip and went on walking.

Sitting on a convenient low bank side by side, they watched a flock of terns picking their way along the waterline, while the dying sun cast a glow of gold over the water. After a time the wind coming off the sea made Briar shiver, and Kynan hauled her to her feet, saying, 'We should be finding a place to eat.'

They were sipping coffee when Kynan said, 'My sister's organised a party for my mother's birthday. Will you come with me?'

'A family party?'

'There'll be friends there, too. My mother is a gregarious soul. I think you'll like her.'

If he was accurate in his guess that she'd prefer the scarf he'd chosen, his mother should be an interesting person. 'Where shall I meet you?' she asked.

He picked her up around the corner from her house. 'Madeline lives on the North Shore,' he told her as he headed for the Harbour Bridge.

'Is your sister married?'

'Yes. She and David have two children. Both boys.'

'So you're an uncle.'

'That's right. You sound surprised.'

'Do you see much of them?'

'My nephews? Not a lot. Occasions like this, and the odd Sunday.'

'Does your mother live with them?'

'She has her own flat in town, but Madeline's place is bigger. That's why the party's over there.'

The two-storeyed weatherboard house overlooked the harbour. A drooping pepper tree and a shaggy-barked pohutukawa shaded the front lawn, and several cars were parked in the driveway.

'Everyone's probably out on the terrace at the back,' Kynan said, 'as it's a nice evening.' The sound of voices and laughter and clinking glasses as he led her along a path to the side of the house indicated he was right. Beyond the tiled terrace, crowded with people, a sloping lawn ended in a stout fence at the top of a steeper slope covered in manuka, orange-flowered flax, and weather-stunted trees. The wind-ruffled water, overlaid with the pink sheen of sunset, was dotted with small craft, and the port was clearly visible on the city side, backdropped by tall buildings, some with lighted windows.

'Uncle Ky!' Two boys aged about five and seven rushed up to him, the smaller one throwing his arms about Kynan's thighs. Kynan ruffled his dark hair. 'This is Jason, and his big brother Duncan. Say hello to Briar, boys.'

They inspected her with interest. 'Hello, Briar.'

Jason confided, tucking his hand in Kynan's, 'Nana says she's a hundred and three, but Duncan says she can't be. Can she, Uncle Ky?'

'If she is, then I'm seventy-one,' Kynan told him. He put his free hand at Briar's waist. 'Come and meet the birthday girl.'

Kynan's mother was as he'd described her, with brown eyes full of laughter, and dark hair unashamedly grey-streaked. She was quite small—her son hadn't got his height from her—and her trim figure was clothed in a smart pair of casual dark red trousers and a hot pink silk shirt. Several fine gold chains unexpectedly combined with a chunky bead necklace completed the outfit.

Briar handed her the cellophane-wrapped flowers she'd bought that afternoon. 'Happy birthday, Mrs Roth.'

'Thank you, there was no need to bring me anything, but these are beautiful.' She took Briar's hand in a firm clasp, and subjected her to a look of friendly interest before putting down the flowers on a chair and opening the parcel that Kynan handed to her.

'Oh, it's *very* nice!' she approved. 'Thank you, Ky.' The boys, after regarding the scarf with mild interest, scampered off to greet another newcomer.

'Briar helped me choose it,' Kynan told his mother. 'I bought it from the shop where she works.'

His mother smiled at Briar. 'Is that how you met?' she asked curiously.

'No, we were properly introduced by her father,' Kynan told her. 'All very respectable.'

'O-oh! Respectable, is it?' She gave him a teasing look. 'Maybe I should take Briar aside and tell her a few stories about how respectable you are!'

He grinned at her. 'Don't you dare. Where's Maddy? And more important, where are the drinks?'

A young woman who could only be his sister appeared at his elbow. Taller than her mother, she had the same brown eyes and wide smile. 'Drinks in the kitchen,' she said. 'David's dispensing. And this is Briar? The boys told me you'd brought a pretty lady along. You do all right for yourself, don't you, bro?'

She grinned up at him, and he roughed up her short dark hair much as he had her son's, saying, 'Enough cheek.'

'Bully.' She dodged away from him, laughing.

Briar watched them with a trace of envy. Lacking brothers and sisters herself, she'd never experienced the particular brand of affection that was palpable between these two.

'Children, children!' their mother admonished. 'Not in front of the grown-ups! Kynan, get Briar something to drink. And you can bring me another Bourbon while you're there, please. Now,' she said, taking Briar's arm in an inexorably friendly grip and pulling her down on to the garden seat beside her, 'tell me about yourself.'

When Kynan returned they were deep in conversation. He handed them glasses and wandered off, coming back some time afterwards to bear Briar off and introduce her to more people.

Later the air cooled and everyone drifted inside, except a dozen diehards who remained on the terrace, dancing to music from a tape player. Most of the time Kynan was at Briar's side, and towards midnight he said in her ear, 'Want to dance?'

She'd had a few glasses of wine by that time, knowing she didn't have to drive. She gave him a slightly muzzy smile and said, 'Sure.'

His answering smile was crooked and for a moment she thought it was just a little calculating. She blinked at him, and he raised his brows, and the calculating look disappeared.

He took her hand and led her outside, to where several couples were swaying to a dreamy tune. Briar hesitated. Minutes ago they'd been dancing to quite different music, with a heavy, insistent beat. After the warmth inside the night air felt cool on her skin.

'Cold?' he said.

'A bit.'

'Dancing will warm you.' Kynan folded her into his arms, and she relaxed against him, sliding her arms up about his shoulders as their feet moved to the rhythm.

Overhead a trellis hung with clematis and wistaria cast intermittent shadows, and in a corner where the shadows were dense and deep one couple had stopped dancing and were kissing instead, their arms wound about each other.

Briar averted her eyes as Kynan guided her past the lovers, and he turned his head, studying them for a second before looking down at her, a smile on his lips.

Briar dipped her head, avoiding his eyes. She felt his arms tighten. She remembered the feel of his lips on hers, and fought down a desire to raise her mouth to him now.

The tape finished, and while someone was replacing it, Briar said, 'I think I'd like to go home, if you don't mind.'

'Tired?'

'A bit. It's been a lovely party. I had a good time.'

He nodded, reluctantly loosening his hold on her. 'I'm glad. Come and say goodnight to my mother.'

Mrs Roth, still talking animatedly with a group of friends, thanked Briar for coming and said warmly, 'I hope to see you again. Get Kynan to bring you round to my place. How about lunch next Sunday?'

'I'll let you know,' Briar promised. 'Thank you.'

'Let her know?' Kynan queried as he let her into the car. 'Don't you want to go to lunch with her?'

'I thought you might not want to be railroaded into taking me.'

He closed the door on her and came round to slide into the driver's seat. 'I'd like to take you,' he said, 'if you think you'd enjoy it.'

'I would. You were right. I like your mother.'

Mrs Roth was an easy, casual hostess whose small flat breathed an atmosphere of liveliness as well as comfort. A collection of family photographs dating from the Edwardian era through to recent colour prints dominated one wall, while on another a large abstract painting took pride of place. Queen Anne occasional tables sat happily alongside art deco chairs, and a perfectly plain rimu coffee-table stood on an antique Chinese rug, all blending in unlikely harmony.

She enlisted their help in the kitchen before lunch, and afterwards led the conversation easily from pollution to flower arranging with a dozen other topics in between.

Briar was enormously entertained, and left reluctantly when it was time to go.

'Are you tired?' Kynan asked her as he started the car.

'No. I had a wonderful afternoon.'

'My mother likes you, too. Do you want to go straight home? Or can I tempt you to eat with me again?'

'This could become a habit,' Briar said lightly.

He turned to look at her, but his eyes seemed veiled. 'Would you object?'

Her father certainly wouldn't. There'd be no trouble in that direction, she thought involuntarily. 'It might be difficult to keep it a secret.'

'Well,' he said, 'let's cross that bridge when we get to it.'

When he took her home he drove right to the house and stopped outside, killing the engine. Then he released her safety-belt and his, and lifted a hand to turn her face towards him.

He studied it for a second or two, and she stirred uneasily, because his gaze seemed remote and almost chilly, although his fingers on her skin were warm and he was so close to her that she could hear the soft sound of his breathing.

Then he leaned forward without haste and kissed her, at first a barely perceptible touching of lips before he withdrew and looked at her again, his hand cradling her cheek. He brushed his thumb across her mouth, and then kissed her properly, tipping her head further back, this time persuading her lips to part for him, and she put a hand on his chest and felt his heart beating strongly against her fingers as she kissed him back.

He moved away and ran one finger down her cheek, and then shifted his hand to the steering wheel. 'Goodnight, Briar,' he said.

She whispered, 'Goodnight,' and slid out of the car. She was shaken by the depth of passion he'd aroused with one relatively chaste kiss. He'd scarcely been touching her, and she'd felt as though she was burning up.

If kissing him became a habit, it could be a dangerous one.

CHAPTER FOUR

NEXT time Kynan arrived at the shop, Briar wasn't surprised. Nor when he asked her if she'd like to attend a film that evening. Afterwards he took her all the way to the doorstep before he kissed her, but when a light went on inside the house he released her immediately and said goodnight, retreating to his car before she opened the door.

Her father was on his way to bed, pausing at the foot of the stairs. 'Been out?' he enquired unnecessarily.

'Yes. A film.'

'Who with?'

Laura would never have asked. Since Briar had reached twenty her stepmother had scrupulously respected her privacy. But Xavier was her father, and saw no reason to give up what he saw as his parental rights.

She said, 'A friend. Where's Laura?'

'In bed. You'd better go to bed, too.'

'I will.' It wasn't so late, but she had work tomorrow, and there was nothing to stay up for. 'I just want a cup of coffee first.' She headed for the kitchen, principally to avoid further questions.

She heard her father's footsteps on the stairs as she opened the fridge and took out a carton of milk. It wasn't just because of Kynan's odd request that she had avoided telling him who she'd been out with. She really wasn't sure why, except that despite his uneasy reassurances she knew he'd been over-anxious for her not to rebuff Kynan.

And she didn't want him looking over her shoulder, asking about or commenting on their seeing each other.

Briar reminded her father of his wedding anniversary as she did every year, and at his request booked a table for him and Laura at a restaurant. She herself accepted an invitation from Kynan that night to a supper show on the other side of town. There was no danger of their bumping into her father and Laura there.

When Kynan took her home they lingered for some time on the doorstep, talking while he absently wound a strand of her hair about his fingers, then touching hands, and finally going into each other's arms. He had his arms wrapped about her waist, and hers were about his neck, her head back until her neck hurt, and she made a small, protesting movement. He didn't relinquish her mouth, but one hand slid up to cradle her nape. He shifted his legs, his thighs warm and strong against hers, bringing her closer still, her body locked so tightly against him that she could feel him breathing, and the stirring of his masculinity. His lips urged hers further apart and she gave him every reaction he silently asked for.

If she hadn't been so lost in the kiss she might have realised that the flare of light wasn't just another car passing on the road. With his arms holding her so close and his mouth intimately exploring hers, the blood pounding in her ears drowned the sound of the car's engine, and it wasn't until the garage door closed and quick footsteps sounded on the path that she stiffened in his grasp and pulled away, whispering, 'My parents!'

She heard his muffled exclamation before he let her go and turned, trapped by the arrival of Xavier and Laura at the foot of the steps.

'Oh!' Laura was startled. 'Mr Roth.'

'Good evening, Mrs Cunningham,' he said smoothly. 'Xavier.' He nodded. 'I was just leaving.'

But Xavier was coming up the steps to meet him. 'No need for us to chase you off,' he said. 'Come inside, have a nightcap with us. We've been celebrating our anniversary. Be a nice way of ending the evening, won't it, my dear?' He turned to Laura.

Laura could only agree, and Kynan gracefully gave in.

'I'll make the coffee,' Laura offered as Xavier steered Kynan into the living-room. Glancing at her step-daughter, she added, 'Come and help, Briar.'

Directly appealed to, Briar had no choice. But as they entered the kitchen, Laura murmured, 'Your lipstick's smudged. I thought you might want to fix it.'

Briar tore off a kitchen towel and wiped her mouth. 'Better?'

'I wish I looked as good without it.' Laura heaped coffee into a filter and placed it in the coffee machine. 'How does Kynan like his coffee?'

'Black.'

Laura shot a smiling look at her, and Briar said resignedly, 'I've been seeing him off and on for weeks. He asked me to keep it quiet.'

'*He* did?'

'Don't ask me why. He didn't say. Except that it isn't because he's married.'

'Maybe he has another girlfriend.' Laura was taking milk from the refrigerator. 'Sorry, I shouldn't have said that.'

'Why not? I don't think that's it. I think . . . he didn't want Dad to know.'

'Well, he knows now.'

Briar could hear the men's voices in the other room, but not the words. 'Yes, he does. I don't suppose it matters.'

When the two women carried in coffee and a plate of cheese and biscuits, Xavier was hunched forward in his chair, apparently making a point to the other man. Briar wondered if the alacrity with which Kynan got up to take the tray of steaming cups from her denoted relief at the interruption.

They talked generally over the coffee, and Briar was surprised when Xavier put down his cup and said, 'Well, I think I'll be off to bed.' He threw a summoning glance at his wife and said affably to Kynan, 'Take your time. Briar will see you out when you're ready. No doubt we'll be seeing more of you.'

Kynan stood up. 'Thanks for the coffee, Mrs Cunningham.'

'Laura,' she said, 'please.' She held out her hand. 'Goodnight.'

When they'd gone he strolled over to the sofa where Laura had been sitting beside Briar, and took her place, laying an arm along the back of it. 'Is your father always so accommodating?' he asked her softly.

Briar put her empty cup on the side table and made to get up, but Kynan hooked his arm about her and turned her to face him. 'You wouldn't disappoint him, would you?'

Briar flushed. 'I'm sure he didn't mean——'

'You know as well as I do what he meant.' And he lowered his mouth to hers, pushing her head back against the sofa, one hand firmly about her waist, the other sliding inside her dress, cupping her breast.

He had never touched her like that before, and there was something about the way he did it now that bothered her, despite the sudden heating of her blood that it caused. She put a hand on his wrist and tried to pull it away, and he lifted his head and said, 'Don't be a prude, Briar.'

She didn't like the way he said it, still less the hard, glittering look in his eyes. Her own eyes bright with anger, she began to struggle in his hold. 'Let me go!'

A flicker of surprise crossed his face. He dropped his hands and stood up, looking down at her. 'What's the matter?'

She didn't really know, except that there was a quality in his lovemaking that hadn't been there before, that made her feel cheapened by his casual caress. She said stiffly, 'I'm not in the mood. I think you'd better go, Kynan.'

He rocked on his heels, thrusting his hands into his pockets. 'Daddy will be disappointed.'

Briar shot to her feet. 'I don't know what you're on about——'

His voice was cutting. 'Don't play dumb, Briar, it doesn't suit you. What I'm trying to figure out is whether you're an innocent pawn, as you claim, or if you've been playing a very clever hand.'

She blinked at him in disbelief. 'You said you believed me——'

'I know. I did—almost. Maybe because I preferred to close my eyes to anything else.'

'*I* haven't been running after *you*!' she said, incensed. He'd made every move, and surely he hadn't forgotten that?

'Not obviously,' he rejoined coolly. 'But you've never run so fast that I couldn't catch you easily enough.'

Her eyes widened with indignation. 'You lousy swine! I didn't set out to *trap* you. Frankly, I wouldn't be bothered! You're not *so* irresistible, you know!'

He laughed, a harsh, caustic sound. 'Not me, perhaps. My money.'

'You are *obsessed*, aren't you?' she accused him.

'With you?' He looked at her with an odd expression, his eyes narrowed and hostile.

Briar shook her head impatiently. 'With the idea that everyone's got an eye to the main chance.'

'It comes from experience. I certainly don't flatter myself that your father set out to make my acquaintance because he thought I'd be nice to know.'

'That's business! It has nothing to do with us—with you and me.'

'Hasn't it?'

Exasperated, she said, 'Even if you're right about my father needing money—all you have to do is say no.'

'I did.'

'You—you mean, he has asked you, and you turned him down?'

'That's what I mean. He was sniffing, sounding me out, before he asked me to dinner here. I wasn't keen, and he knew it. But he pressed the invitation, made it difficult for me to say no without being downright rude. I knew he had something up his sleeve, some kind of extra inducement. I didn't know what it was until I saw you.' Briar gasped, but he didn't seem to notice. 'By then I had done some sniffing of my own and made up my mind to avoid any involvement, but I'd already accepted the invitation. So I came.'

'And then you refused to finance him.'

'Yes. When he came to me with a proposal a few days later, I declined it.'

'Was that why you didn't want him to know that you were taking me out?' Briar asked slowly. 'You were embarrassed?'

'If he thought I'd taken his bait after all, he might have got the impression I could be persuaded to change my mind. I didn't want to raise any false hopes and be put in the position of turning him down again.'

'I'm not *bait*!' She was incensed at the word.

Kynan looked at her consideringly. 'In his mind that's exactly what you are. He took the chance to hint again tonight at a deal between us . . . and you saw for yourself how willing he is to dangle you before me.'

'He was just being . . . tactful.'

Kynan gave a short, disbelieving laugh. 'Face it, Briar. Your father would throw you to the sharks to save his skin.'

'That's not true!'

'It is and I think you know it. Did you plan to make sure I stayed until he got home?'

'How could I have planned it?' Briar demanded. 'I had no idea they'd arrive at the same time that we did!'

'You were very forthcoming tonight. I half expected an invitation to come up to your room.'

Her cheeks burned. It was true she had been passionately reciprocating his kiss, carried away on a tide of pleasure in the feel of his mouth on hers, his arms holding her. But she hadn't planned on anything more than kisses.

He said, 'You kept me there on the doorstep for a good twenty minutes. It was a fairly prolonged goodnight.'

Briar stared at him speechlessly, her anger fading abruptly into a feeling of utter despair. Had he suspected all along that she was carrying out some devious scheme of her father's? Yes, she answered herself, he probably had. He'd never trusted her, in spite of his assurance that he believed her. There had always been a solid core of doubt in his mind, and the slightest evidence was enough to damn her in his eyes.

She said again, 'I think you'd better go.'

He looked at her dispassionately. 'You're probably right. I don't think I'm in the mood for lovemaking tonight, either. You can see me to the door.'

She walked beside him, holding herself rigid, her face a mask.

Kynan opened the front door himself, and stood looking down at her, his expression indecipherable. 'I'll call you,' he said abruptly, and went out without touching her again.

'Don't bother—please.' She shut the door on his retreating back, and leaned on it, fighting a strong desire to weep.

When he phoned her at home, Laura answered, and Briar said, not troubling to lower her voice, 'Tell him I'm out.'

Laura looked shocked, but relayed the message. When she'd put down the phone she said ruefully, 'He said to tell you he knows where you are, and he'll catch up with you another time.'

It sounded like a meaningless social formula, but to Briar it was more like a threat. Every time a tall male customer entered the shop she tensed, only to relax when she found it wasn't Kynan.

But perhaps his message had just been a polite acceptance of her brush-off, after all. Because weeks went by and she didn't see or hear from him. She tried to shake off an unwarranted depression.

* * *

Laura was worried about Xavier. 'He's looking haggard,' she said to Briar. 'And he's working half the night.'

Briar knew it was true. She'd never seen her father appear so worn and old, and the library light was usually burning when she went up to bed. Laura said, 'Could you speak to him, Briar?'

'Speak to him? How? I mean, about what?'

'Ask him what's wrong. He won't talk to me. You know he thinks I'm a fool——'

'I'm sure he doesn't. He thinks women don't know anything about business, that's all.'

'Yes, but he does respect your brain, Briar. He's always saying how sensible and intelligent you are.'

'Really?' Briar blinked in surprise.

'Don't you know? He's very proud of you. Oh, I know he doesn't say so to you, but he is. I think he might tell you—if there's anything we can do to help. When I offer he just says there's nothing to worry about. And there *is*. I know there is.'

'I really don't think he would tell me anything more than he does you.'

'But please try, Briar. For me?'

Laura seldom asked her for anything but the most trivial favours, and there was no way Briar could turn her stepmother down now. She owed her too much.

'All right,' she promised. 'I'll try.'

That evening she waited until Laura had gone to bed, then steeled herself to knock on the library door.

There was no answer, and she opened the door and looked in. What she saw startled her beyond measure. Expecting her father to be bent over a sea of papers, instead she found him sitting behind his desk, gazing unseeingly at the Heaphy picture on the wall, on his face such a deep, tormented despair that she exclaimed, 'Dad! Whatever is it?' And quickly crossed the carpet to kneel beside his chair and take a limp hand in hers.

He looked down at her and seemed to come back from a long way off. 'Briar?' His voice was slow and slurred. His hand in hers felt cold. 'Briar.' He frowned. 'I . . . I'm tired. Ver' tired. Ver' . . . tired.' His eyes looked glazed, and then his head nodded forward on his chest, and she wondered if he'd been drinking.

'Dad?' She looked at him anxiously, cast a glance over the desk, finding no bottle or glass. She put a hand on his forehead, but he didn't seem feverish. 'Can I get you something? Tea—a brandy?'

'Brandy,' he whispered. 'Goo' idea. Goo' girl.' He nodded.

She flew to fetch it, helping him drink it because his hands seemed weak. Making a swift decision, she said, 'I'm phoning the doctor.'

'No . . . I'm a'right. Jus' tired. Tired. I'm . . . all righ'.'

'You're not,' she argued. Something was wrong, and she quickly made the call, relayed her concern, and then ran upstairs to alert Laura.

'A slight stroke,' the doctor diagnosed. 'Make him rest for a few days. I'll get some tests done, and meantime I'll write a prescription. We'll have to keep an eye on his blood-pressure.'

'He's been worried lately,' Laura said. 'Is that what brought it on?'

'Could have triggered it,' the doctor agreed. 'He ought to avoid too much stress. This is a warning. But hopefully it won't happen again.'

* * *

Xavier stayed in bed for a day, grumbling, then insisted that he felt perfectly well and took himself off to the office. Laura could do nothing to stop him.

Then one day Briar came home to find a strange car parked outside.

Laura was hovering in the hallway, wringing her hands. 'Your father came back early from the office with two strange men. He didn't even introduce me to them. They just marched in as though they owned the place. They said something about searching the house!'

'Whatever for?'

'I don't know! They can't be police, can they? Xavier couldn't have done anything criminal! Could he?'

'Where are they now?'

'In the library with him. He looked terrible, Briar, but he wouldn't let me go in there with them. I don't know what to do.'

'I'll try to find out what's going on,' Briar offered. She put down her bag and went to the library, knocked but didn't wait to be invited in.

Her father was standing by the window, his face grey. A man sat in the chair at his desk, riffling through some papers in a drawer which he'd placed on the oak surface. Another man stood by with a notebook in his hand.

'Hello, Dad,' she said, carefully closing the door behind her. 'Laura would like to know what's happening.'

'I'll explain later, Briar.'

'Are you all right?'

'Of course I am.'

Unconvinced, Briar walked forward and spoke to the man at the desk, who had just pulled out another drawer and put it on top of the desk. 'My father has been unwell lately. Don't you need a warrant or something to do that?'

The man fished in his pocket and produced an identification folder, holding it up so she could see. 'We are entitled to ask for full and free access to all documents.'

CHAPTER FIVE

'INLAND Revenue?' Briar stared at the official identification card. 'The Tax Department?'

Xavier said, 'If I don't give consent, they can prosecute.'

The man returned the folder to his pocket. He glanced at Xavier and said, 'You might like to sit down, Mr Cunningham, while we go through this.'

Briar curbed a surge of anger at her father being invited to sit down in his own house while this stranger occupied his chair. After all, the man was only doing his job, and an unpleasant one it was. 'You should, Dad,' she urged.

She thought he was going to refuse, but after a second or two his shoulders drooped, and he walked to one of the leather armchairs and sank heavily into it.

'I'll get you a cup of tea,' she said. Turning to the other two men, she asked coolly, 'Would you gentlemen care for some?'

The man at the desk looked surprised. 'No, but thank you.' The other man just shook his head.

In the hallway Briar told Laura, 'It's something to do with taxes. I wouldn't worry, they're always doing audits and things. Pat had them at the shop a couple of months ago. They'll just be checking, that's all.'

Laura looked relieved, but she said, 'Is Xavier all right?'

'I said I'd take him a cup of tea. He's OK.' She didn't want to send Laura in there, not until he looked better.

When she took in the cup, the men were packing some papers into a box. 'We'll give you a receipt for these, Mr Cunningham, and we'll be in touch. You don't keep any business records anywhere else in the house?'

Xavier shook his head. 'None. I'd appreciate it if you didn't disturb my wife any further.'

The man nodded at him as though satisfied he'd told the truth. 'We'll be going, then. We can find our own way out, thanks.'

But Briar made sure that Laura was still there to see them off before she closed the study door and said, 'Do you have reason to be worried about them, Dad?'

'No, no. Of course not.' But his hand trembled as he lifted the cup to his lips.

She went over to stand near the chair. 'You can tell me,' she said. 'I won't let on to Laura, although I think she ought to know if it's serious.'

He looked up at her, and placed the cup carefully back in its saucer. 'Serious enough,' he admitted. 'If I'd been able to raise that finance—but no one would help me out. Word gets around. I thought that Roth—he hadn't long been in the country, and he might not have heard... Rumours can kill a business, you know. Spread like wildfire.'

He lifted the cup again and took a sip. 'This tax investigation is the last straw. I'll have to sell the house—everything. I'd hoped to save it. Poor Laura.' He shook his head, acute distress in his face. 'There'll be a bankruptcy hearing, and I'll be lucky if...'

Briar sucked in a shocked breath. 'If what?'

'If that's the only court I have to attend,' he mumbled. 'Damn Roth! He was my last chance. I hoped——' He looked up at her, then lowered his head. 'Never mind. It wasn't your fault.'

'Did you...do something wrong?' Briar asked quietly. She felt sick.

Xavier gave a bitter laugh. 'Something unwise. I was playing Peter and Paul, borrowing from one client account, paying it back from another. I got caught short on one investment. It had a domino effect. Then the stories started and clients began asking for their money back before the terms of their investments expired. Plenty of others do the same, but I'm unlucky enough to get caught.'

'The Tax Department?'

'I knew I couldn't pay the tax on my book profits last year. I distributed the income, hoping to defer it. That's not tax evasion, it's avoidance, and legal, but they don't agree. I can't afford to argue the case in court. And now I can't cover my debts.'

'How much money do you need?'

'A few hundred thousand would have pulled me out of the red six months ago. Now...it could be millions.'

Briar suppressed a gasp. 'How many millions?'

'Four...five. I shouldn't have told you this.'

'I would have to know eventually. And so will Laura, if the house has to be sold.' She didn't add that if he was declared bankrupt he could hardly keep that a secret, either.

'Don't tell her yet.'

'No,' Briar said slowly. '*You* should, though. She'll stand by you, Dad.'

'I know. But...she'll lose her respect for me.'

'No!'

'Oh, yes,' he said wearily, and passed a trembling hand over his eyes. 'That's the worst of all this. The one thing I can't stand is that I've failed Laura.'

Briar had never realised that his wife's respect was so important to him, that in his way he really loved Laura. She'd had the impression that he'd married again chiefly in order to provide a mother-figure for Briar and a resident housekeeper. Since she was fourteen and had first indulged in romantic fantasies she'd found it a mystery that Laura could wholeheartedly love her father, who seemed constantly to undervalue her.

There was a tap on the door, and after a moment Laura opened it and stood there, diffidently.

Her father gave Briar an imploring look. She shook her head, reassuring him of her silence, though against her better judgement. She caught a glimpse of Laura sinking down on her knees with her hand on the arm of the chair, before closing the door behind her.

The second stroke was much more severe than the first. Briar received a panic call at the boutique from Laura. Her father had been taken ill at work, and she was phoning from the hospital.

This time Xavier was unable to speak to them for several days, and when he did his speech was impaired. Eventually they were told that they could take him home, but improvement was unpredictable. He was mobile but could move only slowly and with help, and when he talked he had to think before he could force the words out.

'I can nurse him,' Laura declared.

'It'll be tiring,' she was warned. 'Stroke patients can display unpredictable behaviour. You may find he suffers a personality change. You'll need a rest now and then.'

'We can afford help if we need it,' Laura said confidently. 'And my daughter will help, too. Won't you, Briar?'

'Of course.' Briar would do anything to lighten the burden on Laura, but she was wondering if she ought to break the news to her that they couldn't necessarily afford any paid help.

Xavier's secretary came to the house and spent some time conferring with him. Briar saw the young man leave the sick room looking worried.

'Can you understand him?' she asked.

'Oh, yes, mostly. It's not that. I'm just...not sure what I should do about some correspondence that...well, frankly, that I'm afraid might affect him badly.'

'Come into the library and let me see it. You did bring it with you?'

'Yes, but——'

'My father has told me all about his...difficulties. I might be able to help.'

She didn't understand half of it. But she saw enough to say, 'I'm sure you were right not to show him these. Can I keep them for a day or two? I might be able to talk to him by then and make some decisions.'

She was walking across the hall with the papers in her hand, intending to study them in her room, when the phone rang.

She picked up the receiver and recited the number.

'Briar? Kynan here.' He hadn't needed to tell her. She'd recognise those deep tones anywhere, although it was six weeks since she'd heard them. 'I've been told that your father is ill.'

'Yes.'

'Is it bad?'

She told him, briefly, and he said, 'How are you coping?' Then, after a pause, 'And Laura?'

'All right. Laura's tired.' She'd been looking worn and had lost weight, and Briar was worried about her, but the only way she could give her stepmother more help would be to leave her job and stay home to share the nursing. And if the roof was finally about to crash in on their lives, her wages might be the only thing between them and the street.

'You sound tired, too,' Kynan said.

The sympathy in his voice seemed genuine. She felt tears stinging behind her eyes. 'I'm fine,' she said. 'It's kind of you to enquire.'

'Is there anything I can do?'

You could lend us five million dollars. But she couldn't say that. He was making a conventional gesture, offering—what? A short visit to her father, perhaps. A magazine or two. Some small favour.

She looked at the papers in her hand. He'd be able to explain to her the parts she didn't understand, tell her what was meant by the legalese in which the letters and documents were couched, and just how significant were the lawyers' threats of unspecified possible action on behalf of their clients. The secretary, looking like a cornered ferret, had muttered that they were probably not serious. But he'd also said something about being offered another position. The ship was sinking and he didn't intend to be on it when it went down.

'You might...' she began cautiously.

'Yes? Anything, Briar.'

She had to be grateful for that. But...*anything*? Of course he didn't mean it. 'Could I see you some time? Tomorrow, maybe. About...some documents.'

'I'm tied up all day. Will the evening do?'

'Yes, if that suits you.'

'Shall I come round to your place, then?'

She bit her lip. Laura would be about, and Briar had scrupulously kept her promise not to let Laura know anything was wrong with her father's finances. She knew he was keeping the secret as long as possible.

'Or do you want to come to me?' Kynan was saying slowly. 'I can pick you up, if you like.'

'No. No.' She was asking him to do her a favour, after all. 'I'll come to you. Tell me the address.'

He gave it to her and said, 'I'll be looking forward to seeing you.'

After she'd hung up she thought her father would probably not at all like the idea of her discussing his business with an outsider. And had Kynan really meant to offer practical help, or had he just felt obliged to say the expected thing, not for a moment thinking he'd be taken up on it?

And was she simply making an excuse to see him again?

But she did feel she needed expert advice. And he was the only person she knew who might give it without charging some hefty fee she couldn't afford.

He lived in an apartment block. The building was somewhat intimidating, and as the elevator whispered up to the fifth floor she had to fight down a sensation of panic.

The carpet absorbed the sound of her footsteps as she found the number of his apartment and pressed the bell beside the door.

He opened the door almost immediately. She looked up into his face, and her heart momentarily lost its rhythm. His eyes were dark and enigmatic, his expression rather forbidding. She had a sudden urge to turn and run, but he reached out, put a hand on her arm and drew her inside, closing the door.

'Hello,' he said, and smiled at her.

She tried to smile back, but something was making her feel breathless and shaky. She couldn't take her eyes off him, her own wide and almost frightened.

He lifted his black brows and said, 'Something wrong?'

Briar shook her head. The entryway was quite roomy but she felt crowded. 'I'd forgotten how big you are.'

'And I'd forgotten how... beautiful you are.'

He stood looking at her almost broodingly, then abruptly swung round, leading her into a large, airy room with a bank of windows at the far end. The carpet was pale grey, the walls ice-blue. Everything looked expensive but not ostentatious, and there were several original paintings on the walls, two of them heavily framed vistas of misty mountains and bush, the epitome of nineteenth-century romanticism. It crossed her mind that they were a surprising choice for a man like Kynan.

He indicated an air-force-blue leather sofa and said, 'Sit down. Can I get you a drink?'

She nodded, and he didn't ask what she wanted, just mixed her favourite gin-and-lemon from a drinks table in one corner, and poured something for himself before sitting opposite her on a wide chair that matched the sofa.

'How have you been?' he asked softly. 'You look thinner.' His eyes made a leisurely inspection of her, and her pulses quickened when she saw the lambent light in them, the same sensual awareness that she had noticed the very first time they'd met. He still found her attractive, then. She felt a small, primitive pleasure in that.

'It's a bit of a strain,' she said. 'Dad's illness, and . . . everything.'

He nodded.

'It's worse for Laura, though.' She sipped at the cool drink. 'This is good.'

'Will he recover?' Kynan asked.

'He's improved quite a bit, but the doctors can't tell if a full recovery is possible.'

'A stroke, wasn't it?'

'That's right. He had one before——'

'When?' He looked surprised.

She told him, and he said, 'I didn't know.'

'No one did. He went straight back to work afterwards. It was only a small one, but the doctor said it was a warning.'

'Which he didn't heed.'

'He was told to avoid stress. But I don't think that was possible, in the circumstances.'

'Circumstances?'

'He . . . wasn't able to raise the finance he needed for his business, after you turned him down.' She saw a shadow cross Kynan's face and said hastily, 'I'm not blaming you for his illness. Your decision was understandable, especially as . . .' She knew a lot more now than she had, and no one in their right mind would have invested with Xavier if they'd had any idea how badly his affairs were going. 'I know it wasn't a sound proposition,' she said.

'Do you? You gave me the distinct impression that he'd kept you in blissful ignorance.'

Noting the irony in his tone, Briar swallowed. 'Before he became ill he told me how things were. He doesn't want Laura told.' She ignored the brief flash of scorn in his eyes and went on. 'And he mustn't be put under any further stress. That's why I've come to you.'

His gaze sharpened. He lifted his glass to his lips, then lowered it and said, 'And what do you want me to do?'

'You said you'd help,' she reminded him. 'I brought these.' She fumbled in her bag and produced the documents the secretary had left with her. 'I don't quite understand some of them. I hoped you'd be able to explain them to me. And...help me decide what to do.'

He put down his glass on the round coffee-table between them and reached across it to take the papers from her hand. After reading several, he looked up at her. 'Your father's heading for serious trouble.'

Her voice was husky. 'I know that much. The point is, how long before—before something awful happens and—what can I do about it?'

'Why does it have to be you?'

'Because there is no one else.'

His mouth tightened. 'I suppose not.' He looked again at the papers she'd given him. 'My guess is the only reason some of these people are hanging fire is that they know he's ill and they don't want to harass a sick man. Or...they're gathering their forces.'

'For what?'

'At least for requesting an investigation by the securities commission or some other watchdog committee. Or possibly for criminal charges.'

'He's not a criminal!'

'That may be a matter of opinion.'

'Haven't you done similar things in your career? You told me you'd taken a gamble on occasion.'

'Not with other people's money. There's a difference.'

Briar couldn't argue with that. She pleaded, 'But he's *sick*. Facing an enquiry, a court case, might make him worse, even kill him! And there's Laura—she's done nothing wrong. He said they'd have to sell the house.'

'It's a big house for three people.'

Briar looked about. 'This is a big apartment for one.'

'True. But I don't owe a lot of people a lot of money.'

'Anyway, Dad said the proceeds from selling the house wouldn't be nearly enough.'

'How much does he owe altogether? Did he tell you?'

She moistened her lips. 'Four or five million dollars.'

He didn't seem fazed by the amount. He just nodded and said, 'And he doesn't have assets to cover it?'

Briar shook her head. 'Now Laura wants to employ household help, and I've been putting off telling her we can't afford it. She's always looked after the house, but with caring for Dad as well it's become too much. She's working herself to the bone. Next thing, she'll be sick, too.'

'And where will that leave you?'

Briar shrugged. 'I do what I can, but we can't go on like this. And I don't dare stop working. That would only make matters worse, financially.'

'Your wages won't help much.'

'They can't pay off the debts, but they might help to keep us all, if everything else has to go.'

He looked at her thoughtfully. 'Were you hoping to persuade me to change my mind about lending your father some money?'

Briar flushed. 'No! I told you, I needed some advice.'

'My advice would be to tell your father he should throw himself on the mercy of his creditors, plead his state of health and promise to do his utmost to repay what he owes. There's a slim chance he could avoid prosecution and publicity that way.'

She supposed he was right. 'Is there...no other way?'

He tossed off the remainder of his drink, and sat looking down into the empty glass. Then he put it on the table with a small thud and got up to cross to the window and close the slim Venetian blinds against the deepening dusk outside. Briar fought a small tremor of panic. The room seemed very shut in, now.

He turned and looked at her as though debating within himself. Finally he said, 'There is one other way. You could ask me again.'

Dizzy with the hope of a reprieve, she said, 'You'd lend him the money? *Five million dollars?*'

'I said, you could ask me.'

What did he mean? Was he playing some kind of cat-and-mouse game with her? She stared at him, trying to read the masklike expression on his dark features. Perhaps he just wanted to see her humble herself. Maybe he'd get a kick out of saying no. Revenge for her rebuff when he'd phoned and she refused to speak to him.

Pride couldn't enter into this, for her. She had to take the risk. She moistened dry lips and said, 'Would you? Please?'

Some emotion flickered into his face then, and was gone. He thrust a hand into his pocket. 'That depends.'

'On what?'

'On what's in it for me.'

He *was* playing games. Sick disappointment filled her. She wanted to get up and walk away from him. To get away from here, fast. But while there was the slimmest chance to save her father and Laura, she had to stick this out. Her voice low, she said, 'My father hasn't anything worth even half that much to use as collateral.'

'I know he doesn't,' Kynan replied. He came away from the window and walked towards her, standing a few feet away. 'But you do.'

Briar was unable to speak. Her heart pounded as she stared back at him, telling herself he couldn't mean what she was quite sure he did mean.

He said, 'We both know that a loan would be money down the drain. I'd never get it back. But I'll cover his debts, see to it that no one prosecutes him, and buy out his business, on one condition—two, in fact,' he amended.

She was wrong, surely she was wrong. His expression now was totally impersonal. She found her voice. 'What are they?'

'The first,' Kynan said, 'is that he retires from the business immediately and has nothing more to do with handling other people's money. The second...' He paused. 'The second depends on you.'

'Me?' A pulse began hammering in her temple. 'What can you possibly want from me?'

And he said, 'You're not that naïve, surely? You know perfectly well that what I want from you is...you.'

She met his steady gaze, and a slow heat rose through her body to burn in her cheeks. She said, her voice thin against the roaring sound in her ears, 'You're crazy!'

His mouth twitched at one corner. 'Is that your considered opinion?'

Briar shot to her feet. 'Are you seriously offering me five million dollars to...to sleep with you?'

His eyes narrowed. He regarded her flushed, outraged face and said, 'The point is, would you?'

She opened her mouth to shout, *No!* And then she thought of Laura's increasingly haunted eyes, and her father's ravaged face and body. She stifled her anger and the other emotion that lay under it, a kind of nauseated grief. 'It's a...very high price to pay,' she said huskily.

A leaping flame seemed to come and go in his eyes. He put out a hand and his fingers lay against her cheek, his thumb lifting her chin. 'Don't you think you're worth it?'

Her senses leapt under his touch. Despising him, despising herself, she said, 'You're the one making the offer.'

'And are you accepting it?'

Her heart was beating so fast and hard she could scarcely speak. 'I need...to know exactly what the terms are.' He wasn't, surely, going to pay that kind of money for one night of sex. Was he saying he wanted her as his mistress? For how long? Until he tired of her, she supposed.

I can't do it, she thought. I *can't*. One night or a hundred, it made no difference. She'd be reducing herself to the level of a prostitute. Her lips parted, ready to refuse his grotesque proposition, to return them both to sanity, but he suddenly dropped his hand from her face and swung away from her. 'Right,' he said. 'Terms.' Turning to face her, he spoke crisply. 'Contrary to your rather fevered imaginings, Briar, I'm not suggesting I buy your beautiful body for a night—or even several nights.'

A great wave of relief swept over her, but she looked at him in bewilderment. 'You said——'

'That I want you. Oh, yes. And your reply was...interesting.' His gaze flicked over her, and she shivered. He smiled, a grim curving of the lips. 'As you said, I'm offering a high price for what I want. And what I want—is a wife.'

CHAPTER SIX

'A *WIFE*?'

'That never occurred to you?' He looked savagely amused now. 'You were willing to sell yourself cheap, Briar. Not a good bargainer, are you?'

She whitened. It had certainly never occurred to her that he was talking about marriage. Why should it? She said aloud, 'I didn't think that you'd need to buy yourself a bride.'

He gave a short, unamused laugh. 'The thought hadn't crossed my mind before tonight, but it goes against the grain to give money away for nothing unless it's to a deserving charity. Your father doesn't quite come into that category, I'm afraid.'

Briar winced. 'You're not serious, are you? You've just been having fun at my expense. I hope you enjoyed yourself.' She bent to scoop up the papers he'd left on the table, and stuffed them into her bag. Her hands were shaking. 'I'll be going now. Sorry to have wasted your time.'

As she straightened, he said calmly, 'I'm perfectly serious. It's quite usual in a number of countries for a man to pay a bride price to her family. And it's not so long since a woman's father was expected to provide a dowry in our society. Money or goods changing hands at marriage is a time-honoured custom all over the world.'

'And governments all over the world are trying to stamp out the practice.'

'Where it's been abused, certainly. The point is, I'm willing to do for my father-in-law something I wouldn't do for a mere business acquaintance.' He thrust his hands into his pockets. 'I'm sorry I'm not altruist enough to hand over several million dollars free and gratis out of sheer goodness of heart. I do want something in return. And a night or two of passion isn't enough. Oh, I want you in my bed—that goes without saying. But I also want you at my side—as a companion, a hostess, a partner, if you will. Someday I'd like you to have my children.'

'Your children?'

'You're healthy and good-looking,' he said coolly. 'And intelligent. You seem to have some kind of protective instinct about your nearest and dearest. That's an essential ingredient of motherhood, I'd say. I'm ready to get married, have a family. You have all the necessary qualifications.'

'What about love?' This conversation couldn't be happening. Nobody could be that cold-blooded, talking about marriage and motherhood as though they were nothing more than a business transaction.

'Plenty of people marry without love,' Kynan said. 'It's the way things were done for centuries, and still are in many cases. I don't believe marriages of convenience are statistically less successful than those that start in a romantic haze. We have a lot in common—including sexual compatibility, if those kisses we shared are any indicator. I see no reason why marriage shouldn't work for us.'

Briar said slowly, 'You *are* serious!'

'Totally.'

'And you are crazy!' she reiterated.

He smiled suddenly. She found it oddly reassuring, as though they had returned to the time, weeks ago, when he would stroll into the shop and ask her to come with him for a drink, or dinner, and they'd sit and talk for several hours before he took her home and kissed her with barely restrained passion on the doorstep.

He said, 'Only mildly.' He reached out and took her left hand in his, looking down at the slim, ringless fingers. 'Briar,' he said, lifting his head to capture her eyes with his, 'will you marry me?'

And she heard herself say, 'Yes.'

Afterwards she thought he must have infected her with some kind of madness. She couldn't really have agreed to marry a man for the price of five million dollars. Could she? And equally, he couldn't really have made that bizarre offer—could he?

Immediately she'd said the fatal word accepting him, she wanted to retract it, attacked by a paralysing awareness of the enormity of what she was doing. And frightened of what might follow.

But Kynan just said, 'Thank you,' and raised the hand that he still held to his lips. She felt the momentary brush of his mouth over her fingers, and then he released her.

'Sit down,' he said, and she did, because for one thing her legs felt weak. He took a couple of steps away from her and turned to face her again, his voice dispassionate. 'I'll have my lawyers draw up an agreement.'

'An ... agreement?'

'A marital contract. You won't object if I ask you to waive your entitlement to half my estate in the event of a divorce, in favour of an immediate settlement of five million?'

Stiffly, Briar shook her head. 'No, I won't object.' Did he intend to divorce her? But he'd said he wanted children. Surely he wasn't planning a temporary arrangement?

As if he'd read her mind, he said, 'Don't get me wrong. I intend this marriage to last. For my part, I'll do my utmost to see that it does. But I also don't want to find myself being taken to the cleaners in the event that you decide otherwise.'

'I wouldn't——'

'Maybe not. It's a safeguard. And,' he paused, 'I'd want custody of any children if the marriage broke up for any reason.'

'*No*!' Her refusal was instinctive and unequivocal.

His dark brows rose. 'Do I need to remind you that I hold all the cards here?'

Her chin lifted. 'I don't care how many cards you hold. *No one* is going to take my children from me!'

He laughed. 'You don't even have any, yet!'

'*You* said you wanted . . . wanted me to have children.'

'My children.'

'They'll be mine too. You can't treat me like some brood mare, Kynan! I won't agree to that. Not for a *hundred* million dollars! No woman would accept it! If you insist on it the deal's off.'

He regarded her silently for several seconds. Then he said, 'OK. Joint custody. And an independent arbitrator to sort out the details of how it's to be done. Will that suit you?'

Reluctantly, Briar nodded. This whole thing was unreal. Any minute now she'd wake up and find she'd been having some insane sort of nightmare.

But she hadn't. She drove home in a daze, let herself into the house and said goodnight to Laura and her

father who were watching television, then went to bed.
And lay for hours trying to fathom Kynan's motives.

He wasn't in love with her, she was sure. He'd liked
taking her out and was physically attracted, but had never
really believed that she had no ulterior motive in continuing to see him. Tonight had probably reinforced that
opinion. She'd assured him that all she wanted was his
advice, but wasn't it true that deep down she'd nursed
a faint hope that he might be generous enough to save
her father from the consequences of his folly?

Well, he was willing to do that, but he was exacting
a price for it. A very high price.

So what was in it for him? Marriage to a woman he
didn't quite trust, but whom he thought would enhance
his life. He wanted a wife, he'd said, a companion,
hostess, housekeeper, she supposed...and he wanted her
to give him children.

A wave of heat swept over her. He wanted a bedmate,
too. A sexual partner. He might not be in love with her,
but he'd made no secret of the fact that he'd like to take
her to his bed.

She'd half expected him to insist on it tonight. But
he'd scarcely touched her again. Hadn't even kissed her
before she left his flat, or after escorting her down to
the street where she'd parked. Perhaps he'd guessed that
his talk of contracts and arbitrators had chilled any
possibility of response from her.

In the past she'd found his kisses exciting. She couldn't
deny that. She'd found him stimulating to be with, even
liked him after she'd got over her initial anger when he'd
so totally misunderstood her. Occasionally she'd wondered if she was falling in love with him, if the lifting
of her spirits when she saw him and the sharp depression

she felt each time he casually left without arranging another date were symptoms of a dawning love.

She'd wisely repressed those feelings, deliberately kept them in check because she was sure that he was in no danger of losing his head—or his heart. His random invitations when he was at a loose end and had nothing better to do didn't argue any serious involvement.

For all she knew he might have been giving similar invitations to several other women. He'd never attempted to take their physical relationship much further than those seductive goodnight kisses. And when she'd refused his phone call, far from worrying about having offended her, or engaging in any hot pursuit, he'd made no further effort to contact her until his innate good manners had prompted a polite enquiry after her father's health.

So it was only the fact that she was suitable for his purposes and conveniently compelled to put herself in his debt that had led him to propose to her.

By morning, waking muzzily from a restless and too-short sleep, she'd decided to call Kynan and tell him the whole thing was off. He'd probably be relieved. Hadn't he said last night that the idea had only just occurred to him? It had been an aberration on his part, a spur-of-the-moment thing that he probably hadn't meant at all. She should have laughed it off and left.

Before she got a chance to call him, he phoned her. 'I'll pick you up at lunchtime,' he said. 'I've contacted my lawyer and told him what we want. He'll have something ready for us to sign.'

She took a deep breath and said, 'Don't you think this has gone far enough?'

There was a small silence before he said, 'What are you talking about?'

'I called your bluff,' she said, 'but I won't hold you to it. The joke's over, Kynan.'

'Bluff?' he queried sharply. 'I wasn't bluffing, Briar. And you didn't think it was a joke last night.'

She was biting her lip. 'But surely——'

'But nothing,' he said flatly. 'You've got cold feet, is that it?' His voice suddenly altering to a deeper and almost coaxing note, he added, 'Stop worrying. I'll see you at lunchtime.'

When he did, he ushered her into his car and then turned to take both her hands in his, holding them firmly. 'Look at me, Briar.'

She met his eyes, and he said, 'I meant what I said last night, and I don't believe you thought anything else at the time.' He paused. 'At least it's an honest transaction. Would you have found it easier if I'd said "Sure I'll give you the money, no strings attached—and by the way, will you marry me"?'

Reluctantly, she shook her head. Put that way, there wasn't a lot of difference. She'd have felt obligated either to say yes, or to refuse the money. At least he'd been open with her about wanting something in return.

'Right, then,' he said. 'It won't be so bad, you know.' And he lifted one hand to tilt her chin, pressing a lingering kiss on her mouth, which she found she was quite unable to return. Withdrawing, he added drily, 'Do you think you could try to look a little less like Mary Queen of Scots on her way to her execution?'

Signing the document the lawyer placed in front of her, Briar experienced a sensation of inevitability. The man had been briskly formal until then, but perhaps something in her face made him say, 'It may seem to take some of the romance out of things, but a pre-nuptuil agreement is simply a sensible precaution—like an insurance policy. We all hope that it will never have to be used, but, if the worst should happen, it saves a lot of trouble and heartache.'

She nodded, watching Kynan add his signature to the three copies with a decisive scrawl. When they returned to the street she said, 'Thank you for being so...generous.' The final draft had included not only an allowance for herself in the event of a divorce initiated by him, but a lifetime annuity for her father and stepmother.

'I thought it might make you feel more secure,' he said. 'Now,' he glanced at his watch, 'we have about half an hour to find an engagement ring.'

'Engagement ring? I don't want——'

'It's usual, isn't it? We *are* engaged, Briar. I want you to wear my ring. We'll choose a wedding-band, too. It won't be long before we'll be needing it. Will three weeks suit you?'

'*Th-three weeks*?'

He looked at her curiously. 'Your father,' he reminded her gently, 'can't afford to wait too long. If you're worried that people might think we're marrying with unseemly haste, they'll soon discover their mistake, won't they? You won't be pregnant on your wedding-day.'

'Does that mean you——?'

'It means,' he spelled out, 'that as the contract states, your father gets his money on the day that you marry me. And I get you. Not before. Quid pro quo.'

'Do you have to be so——?'

'Crude? Sorry if I've offended you. I'll try to be more sensitive.'

He must have made arrangements beforehand to view rings, because he only murmured his name to the sales assistant in the plush jeweller's shop he took her to, and they were immediately shown into a private room. Several trays of rings were brought to them one by one, and there wasn't a price tag in sight.

'I don't know,' Briar said. 'They're all very beautiful.' She felt suffocated in the small room, and the glittering stones seemed to dance before her eyes. 'You choose,' she said to Kynan.

But when he picked up a huge diamond solitaire she said hastily, 'Oh, no! Not that one. It's too big.'

'The lady has a dainty hand,' the assistant said. 'How about this one?' She held up a thin gold band with a sparkling diamond flanked by two smaller dark pink garnets.

'Try it on,' Kynan urged her. 'You like garnets, don't you?'

She'd been wearing her garnet earrings the first time they met. Did he, too, remember every tiny detail of that evening?

Briar slipped the gold circle on to her finger. It fitted perfectly and Kynan picked up her hand, inspecting it. 'How do you feel about it?'

'It's . . . fine.' Feeling something more was expected of her, she tried to inject some enthusiasm into her voice. 'Lovely.'

'We'll take it,' he told the assistant. 'We need to choose a wedding-band to go with it. Plain gold, don't you think, darling?'

He smiled at Briar and she looked at him wordlessly, stupidly shocked by the endearment. The assistant disappeared through the curtained doorway, and Kynan said, 'If you fancy something more elaborate——'

'No. No, anything you like.'

She thought he was faintly annoyed, but he didn't say any more until the woman came back with a selection of wedding-rings. 'Are you going to wear one too, sir?' she asked him.

'Would you like me to?' he asked, turning to Briar.

Some complicated emotion churning inside her, she raised her eyes to his and boldly said, 'Yes.'

To her surprise, he looked almost pleased. 'OK,' he told the woman. 'Matching rings.'

When the woman asked if she wanted to wear the engagement ring or have it put in a box, Briar said hastily, 'A box, please.'

Kynan took charge of it, along with the wrapped package that contained the wedding-rings.

Outside she said, 'I'm going to be late back.'

'Only a couple of minutes. Will Pat fuss?'

He wouldn't, but she'd found all this more of an ordeal than she'd expected. 'I just don't like to take advantage,' she temporised.

As he let her out of the car he said, 'I'll pick you up after work. Have you told your parents yet?'

Briar shook her head. She didn't know how she was going to approach the subject.

'We'll tell them together, if you like,' he said. 'I'll ask your father for your hand.' He grinned at her and waved as she stood on the pavement watching him drive off.

'I'm expecting a visitor after dinner,' Briar told Laura. 'Will you and Dad be ... around?'

'Of course we'll be home.' Xavier wasn't well enough yet to go out. 'But if you want us out of the way——'

'No,' Briar said hastily. 'No, I meant . . . he wants to speak to you. To Dad, anyway.'

'He?' Laura looked alert and interested.

'Kynan Roth,' Briar explained. 'I'm going to marry him, Laura.'

The words sounded strange, and she immediately wanted to call them back. 'Don't say anything to Dad,' she added. 'Kynan will—we'll tell him tonight.'

Laura said, 'I'm sure he'll be pleased. I thought you weren't seeing Kynan any more.' Then she smiled and stepped forward to hug her stepdaughter. 'I hope you'll be very happy, Briar. How lovely to have some good news for a change!'

Laura's pleasure made Briar feel a little better. Obviously she didn't think there was anything strange or unusual about the engagement. And Briar certainly wasn't going to confide the real reasons to her.

Briar met Kynan at the door and let him in. He caught her shoulders briefly and brushed a quick kiss across her cheek.

'Have you told them yet?' he asked.

Briar shook her head. 'Laura knows. Not my father. Come in, they're waiting.'

She led the way to the small sitting-room that her mother had made into a comfortable TV room, the set hidden in a cabinet specially designed to blend with furniture suited to the vintage of the house.

Laura rose to greet him, smiling as she offered him both her hands. 'How nice to see you again, Kynan. Do sit down.'

He kissed her cheek much as he had Briar's, and turned to Xavier, sitting stiffly in a large armchair.

'I'm sorry about your illness,' he said. 'Briar tells me you're getting better.'

'Slowly,' Xavier agreed. His voice had lost its normal strength, and his speech was measured, as though he had to think of every word before uttering it. 'Laura...says...you wanted to see me.'

'Yes.' Kynan held out his hand to Briar and drew her down beside him on the sofa. 'We want you and Laura to be the first to know that Briar has agreed to be my wife.'

'Briar?' Her father looked at her in obvious surprise. 'I...had no idea.' His gaze passed to Kynan. 'When...did this happen?'

'Last night,' Kynan replied. 'I hope you'll be pleased.'

'Pleased.' He repeated the word as if he were trying it out. 'Well...this is...unexpected.' A hint of colour came into his sallow cheeks. 'Pleased. Yes...I'm pleased. Congratulations.'

'Thank you.' Kynan turned a tight smile on Briar at his side. 'And now that I've gained her consent, I don't want to give her a chance to change her mind. We thought we'd get married quite soon.'

Laura said, 'How soon?'

'Three weeks,' Kynan said calmly. 'You don't want a big wedding, do you, darling?' he asked Briar.

She moistened her lips. 'No. Dad isn't well enough...'

'It's awfully soon,' Laura objected.

Xavier was frowning. 'Is...there some reason...for haste?' he asked.

'There is no reason for delay,' Kynan said shortly.

Laura looked from one man to the other and said, 'Briar, why don't we go and get some coffee?'

Briar rose and followed her. 'I'm not pregnant,' she said as they entered the kitchen. 'It's just that Kynan is...rather impatient.'

'Bless you, Briar, I never thought you were! And I'm sure your father doesn't, either. All the same, don't let Kynan rush you if you're not certain you're doing the right thing. If he loves you, he'll wait.'

But he doesn't, and Dad's creditors won't wait, Briar thought bleakly. Not for much longer. 'I don't want to wait,' she said aloud, hoping that she sounded like a girl in love and eager for her wedding-day. 'There's no point.'

When they returned to the other room, Xavier was looking thoughtful, casting Briar a sharp glance as she came in, but Kynan seemed perfectly relaxed.

Laura said, 'We should be having champagne instead of coffee, really. This is a celebration, after all.'

A shadow crossed Xavier's face, but then he looked at his wife and said carefully, 'Later...my dear.'

It occurred to Briar that his attitude towards Laura had softened since his illness. And in some strange way Laura, despite the obvious worry that it had caused her, seemed happier.

One thing, she thought, there was going to be no pressure on Laura to entertain Xavier's business friends any longer, even if he fully recovered. Kynan had made it clear that a condition of settling her father's debts would be that he gave up his business interests. For Laura that could only be a blessed relief.

'Perhaps,' Kynan suggested, 'we could all celebrate with a dinner out one night. And crack open a bottle or two of champagne.'

'That would be nice!' Laura smiled at him. 'But I don't know if Xavier can stand up to it.'

'Of course...I can,' Xavier said. 'Time I...got going.'

'The doctor said——'

'Damn...the doctor!' He sounded almost like his old self. 'Can't rot...in a chair...the rest of...my life.'

'Well, if you're careful,' Laura agreed.

'Don't...fuss...Laura!'

'Yes, all right,' she said quickly. 'I don't suppose it will do any harm.'

Kynan said, 'I'm sure it won't. You needn't drive. I can pick you all up, and if Xavier needs help—I've got strong arms.'

'I...only need...one,' Xavier told him. 'I'm not...a wheelchair case.'

'That's good.' Kynan smiled easily. 'I'll book a table, then.'

When he rose to leave he held out his hand to Briar and drew her with him to the front door. 'Come and sit in the car for a minute,' he said.

She got in beside him, suddenly shy in the confined space. He drew a ring box out of his pocket and said, 'Time you put this on. Give me your hand.'

He held it in a light clasp as he pushed the ring gently on to her finger.

'Thank you,' she said stiltedly. 'I do like it.' It was a beautiful ring, and in normal circumstances she'd have been enraptured by it. Only the circumstances weren't normal, and she kept feeling small waves of panic at what she was doing.

'I'll put a notice in the paper,' he said. 'Your father and I agreed.'

'Did you tell him...you were going to settle his affairs? And that...you want him to give up the business?'

'Yes. He didn't object.'

His tone was dry, and she sent him a fleeting glance. 'I'm sure he's grateful. Do we really need an engagement notice?'

'I think so. If nothing else it may keep your father's creditors away for a bit longer, until they see which way the wind is blowing.'

'I see.' She supposed they would guess that Kynan Roth wouldn't relish a financial scandal breaking about his father-in-law. But they could surely have no idea of the extent of the rescue mission he had undertaken. 'I'm grateful,' she told him. 'Really.'

'You needn't be,' he said rather roughly. 'You're giving me something in return.' He paused. 'Is it worth it?'

She looked at him fleetingly. 'I...hope so. And I don't suppose many women would balk,' she admitted, 'at the price. My father said once——'

'Said what?' he prompted, as she paused.

'That you were a very good catch,' she finished reluctantly. 'He didn't mean——'

'I've a fair idea what he meant. Do *you* think I'm a good catch?'

Of course he was. Rich, handsome, with no known vices. She said, 'You know the answer to that.'

'Do I?' But he didn't press her any further. 'I'd like to kiss you goodnight, Briar. Do you mind?'

He'd never asked for permission before. Not that she'd ever objected. She lifted her face to him.

But he didn't kiss her right away. He sat looking down into her eyes as if trying to read her mind, then brushed her cheek with the back of his fingers before threading them into her hair and tilting her head further before his mouth came down to hers.

It was a thorough kiss of concentrated sensuality and it should have roused her to an answering passion.

Instead she found herself shrinking inside, her heart growing cold and dead within her. After a while he stopped trying to urge a response from her, and lifted his head, his hand shifting to her throat. His breath was audible, and he said harshly, 'What is this? Reprisal?'

'I don't know what you mean,' she answered. 'I'm sorry...I just can't...'

'Can't? Or won't?' His eyes glittered. Without waiting for an answer he kissed her again, and this time there was no vestige of tenderness in it and no mercy.

When his hand slid from her throat to lie heavily on her breast, she began to struggle, pushing away from him, ending with her back against the door, her eyes wide and her mouth parted with her quickened breathing.

They stared at each other across a couple of feet of space, and he put a hand blindly on the steering wheel, gripping it hard. 'I apologise,' he said, his voice husky. 'I had no right to do that.'

'I thought that was the whole point,' she said. 'You do have a right, don't you? In future I'll try to remember, and make sure you get...what you're paying for.'

'Briar——'

But Briar had already scrambled out and slammed the door behind her. She ran up the path to the house as though the devil himself were after her.

CHAPTER SEVEN

SHE didn't see Kynan again until he called for her and her parents to take them to dinner. Briar had dressed carefully in rose chiffon with a low neckline and floating cape-like sleeves. She wore her garnet earrings and Kynan's ring.

Laura let him in as Briar was coming down the stairs, and when he looked up at her she experienced a feeling of *déjà vu*. But this time he came to the foot of the stairs and waited for her to join him, while Laura with a little laugh retreated to the sitting-room, saying, 'Join us for a pre-dinner drink when you're ready, you two.'

Kynan was standing with his hand on the polished rail where it curved into a decorative whorl at the end. Briar stopped when her eyes were level with his.

'You're very lovely,' he said. 'I'm a lucky man.'

You're a wealthy man, she thought, biting back the remark. Wealthy enough to buy almost anything—even me. She shivered.

'Is that dress warm enough?' he asked.

'I'm not cold.' She probably wouldn't need the woollen wrap that hung over her arm.

He said, 'Do I frighten you?'

'Of course not.' She met his eyes unflinchingly. She was frightened, but he'd never given her cause to fear him physically. Even that last time he'd kissed her so fiercely, she would never have escaped his hold unless he'd allowed her to. Her trepidation was caused by nervousness at the thought of the enormous step she was taking in marrying him—a marriage without love.

He said, 'Good.' And stepped back, allowing her to descend the last stair. As she turned to go along the hallway to the sitting-room his hand rested at her waist. It seemed to burn through the thin material of her dress.

'Your father's creditors have agreed to a month's grace,' he told her.

'You've seen them all?'

'Spoken to them. You've nothing to worry about now.'

Nothing? she thought hysterically. 'Thank you,' she managed to say, just as they reached the door of the room.

Laura had already poured drinks for Xavier and herself. Briar asked for a glass of dry sherry, and after a moment's hesitation Kynan opted for the same.

'To...the happy...couple,' Xavier intoned, raising his glass in a slightly unsteady hand.

Briar felt Kynan's arm go around her shoulders, and looked up to see him gazing down at her with faint mockery in his eyes. 'To us,' he said softly, touching his glass to hers before tipping back his head to drink. She found herself watching with fascination the taut, lightly tanned skin of his throat as the muscles moved beneath it, and it wasn't until he'd lowered his glass and looked questioningly at her that she raised hers.

Kynan helped Xavier into the back seat of the car beside Laura, and opened the front passenger door for Briar. At the restaurant Xavier declined the other man's arm when they left the vehicle, and leaned on Laura's instead. Once at the table he was able to manage quite well, with Laura's help to cut up his steak.

Watching them, Briar speculated on just why Laura had married her father. His motives she'd always thought obvious enough. He'd had a motherless child and a large house, a business to run and the necessity of entertaining in the course of it. Neither the child nor the house had thrived on the desultory and detached care of a succession of housekeepers. Laura had been his solution— as far as Briar was concerned, a brilliant one. Starved for expressions of love and still missing the mother she'd lost two years before, she'd had no reservations at all about accepting Laura as a substitute.

But what had Laura got out of it?

'Briar?' Kynan's deep voice recalled her wandering thoughts. 'Do you want more champagne?' There was some left in the second bottle that still reposed in an ice bucket on the table.

Briar shook her head. She'd drunk enough already to make her light-headed. She'd felt it would help her keep up the appearance of a newly engaged girl without a care in the world. 'Just coffee,' she said. 'I think I need it.'

He smiled and ordered coffee. 'Your father's looking tired,' he said quietly as she finished it. 'I think we should take him home.'

Xavier had fallen silent and his head was drooping on his chest. Briar noticed that Laura was unobtrusively holding his hand in hers. As Kynan got to his feet, Laura brushed a lock of greying hair back from Xavier's forehead. 'Come on, dear,' she said gently, 'time to go.' She bent to help him up.

'I'll do it,' Kynan said, moving swiftly to the older man's side. This time Xavier made no demur.

*   *   *

When they got home Kynan helped Xavier to his room, with Laura behind them. Then he came back to Briar, waiting for him in the hall. 'It's still quite early,' he told her. 'Do you want to go out again, to a club or...?'

Briar shook her head. 'No.' After a tiny pause she added, 'But you don't have to go yet, if you'd rather not. We could...listen to some music or something.'

He smiled wryly. 'The "or something" sounds promising,' he said. 'What did you have in mind?'

She looked away. Before they became engaged she had enjoyed his kisses, his mild lovemaking. And she'd had no problem talking to him. Now she seemed tongue-tied in his presence, and whenever he came near her her emotions seemed to freeze and she tensed, afraid of not being able to meet his demands—demands that surely he was entitled to make.

Kynan gave a short, unpleasant laugh. 'I think I get the message,' he said. 'No payment before the due date, is that it?'

Shocked, she opened her mouth to protest, but he didn't wait for her to speak. His hand was hard under her chin, his mouth almost as hard on her parted lips, but only for a second. Then he was saying, 'Call that a little something on account.' And before she could recover her poise, he'd pulled open the door and closed it again behind him.

The following Sunday he took her again to his sister's house. Madeline had invited her mother and some other relatives and made a family party of it.

On the way there Briar said, 'It wasn't what you thought, the other night. Only...I find the situation a bit difficult sometimes. I don't intend to cheat you, Kynan.'

He cast her a rather remote glance. 'Just try not to let my family know how difficult you find it, will you? I'd like them to think of this as a normal engagement.'

'So would I!'

'Well, then it's rather up to you to convince them of that, isn't it?'

'There are two of us involved in this,' she reminded him.

'Don't worry,' he said. 'I'll play my part to the hilt.'

He did, emerging from the car to hook an arm about her waist even before the family noticed their arrival. It was a minute or two before his two nephews, followed by Madeline and her mother, came flying out to greet them.

The two women kissed and hugged Briar, and she couldn't help but feel both warmed and slightly guilty at their obvious delight.

Kynan remained at her side all the afternoon, holding her hand, sitting with an arm draped along the sofa back behind her, pulling her close when Madeline produced a camera and told him to 'Hold her hand so we can see the ring.'

David, standing beside his wife, added, 'Give her a kiss, Ky. We'll record the moment for posterity. Pucker up, Briar.'

Only Briar could see the sardonic look in Kynan's eyes as she raised her mouth to his. He made the most of it, kissing her until Duncan and Jason began making small-boy 'Yuk! Yu-uk!' noises. Their mother scolded them for rudeness and David, grinning, called, 'Cut!'

Flushed, Briar drew away, fixing a determined smile on her face. Kynan retained an arm about her waist, smiling too. 'All right,' he said. 'Show's over for today.'

Madeline served a lavish afternoon tea, and then most of the guests departed, but Mrs Roth and Kynan and Briar had been invited to stay for dinner. Madeline murmured something about things to do in the kitchen.

'Let me help,' Briar volunteered. She slipped away from Kynan's casual hold and followed her hostess. 'What can I do?'

'Make a coleslaw if you like. The ingredients are all here,' Madeline said, while she took a cold roast chicken from the fridge and picked up a serrated knife.

The two boys came in claiming starvation, and Madeline routed them with reminders of how much chocolate cake and how many muffins they'd had and, when that failed to work, a wave of the knife in her hand accompanied by threats of undefined retribution if they didn't scarper at once.

'Brats,' she said when they'd gone, returning to her attack on the chicken. 'Are you and Kynan planning a family? Believe me, you may live to regret it.'

Well aware that she didn't mean it, Briar smiled. 'Not immediately,' she said. 'But Kynan—we—do want to have children some day.'

'He's good with kids,' his sister said. 'Better with kids than with women.'

'I find that hard to believe,' Briar said. When she'd first seen him she'd got the impression he was a man who knew far too much about women.

Madeline grinned. 'Well, I suppose you would.'

Briar placed a pile of thinly sliced cabbage in the glass bowl Madeline had given her. 'I rather thought he was something of an expert.'

'Oh, I'm sure he makes love wonderfully, but that's not all there is to a relationship. He's always kept his women rather at arm's length—metaphorically speaking. Kynan has a problem with intimacy.'

Briar, slicing into some more cabbage, paused and looked up.

Madeline looked guilty. 'Look, I shouldn't have said that. David says I read too much pop psychology. Maybe he was just waiting for the right girl to come along. He'd never have kissed any of his other girlfriends like that, in front of the whole family. He's in love with you, which is wonderful, and that's all that really matters, isn't it? Let me tell you, we're all bloody grateful. I've been hoping for a sister-in-law for years, and Mum can stop feeling guilty——'

'Why should she feel guilty?'

'Oh, well, her divorce and all, you know. It hit Kynan worse than me, somehow. Being a girl, I was closer to Mum anyway, and Kynan was at a vulnerable age.'

'I thought your mother was a widow.'

'Technically speaking. Only she was a divorcee first. Dad went off with a dolly-bird when we were just kids. Teenagers, anyway. I was scarcely even that.'

'How old was Kynan, then?'

'Fifteen. He took it hard. Dad wanted him to visit, and offered him a place in the business when he left school, but Kynan didn't want any of it. After the dust had settled and they'd got married he did go and stay with them on holidays, but it wasn't a success. We were really surprised when Dad left him the business after all, plus some money to my mother and me. The new wife wasn't pleased, but the court said she'd done all right and they weren't inclined to interfere.'

'She contested the will? That must have been unpleasant.'

'Mmm. It was only finally resolved a few months ago. Poor Kynan——'

'Why? He won, didn't he?'

Madeline paused, her dark eyes flashing. 'After the judgement was given he went to see her—I think with some idea of burying the hatchet. I saw him afterwards and he looked *sick*. I don't know what the rotten bitch said to him——' Madeline sawed viciously at the chicken. 'He wouldn't tell me. But that's Kynan. Just clams up.'

'I thought you seemed close,' Briar told her.

'We've always got on well. But he's the sort who keeps his problems to himself. You must have noticed that? Or has he opened up to you?'

Briar smiled, murmuring something she hoped sounded convincing. 'There were no children involved—from the second marriage?'

'No, thank goodness.' Madeline speared a piece of the chicken and transferred it to another plate. 'Well, she's still a good-looking woman. She'll probably find some other sucker, if she gets through all the money that Dad left her. She was a lot younger than him.'

As the car climbed the high hump of the Harbour Bridge on the way home, Briar said, 'I hadn't known your parents were divorced.'

Kynan cast her a frowning glance. 'Who mentioned that?'

'Madeline. She said you were cut up about it at the time.'

'Madeline exaggerates. I'd almost forgotten about all that.' He glanced into the rear-view mirror and smoothly changed lanes. 'It's not important, Briar. Forget it.'

'Did you see much of your father? Madeline said you stayed with him and his new wife, once.'

'Once.' He laughed suddenly.

Briar cast him an enquiring glance.

'She "didn't want to come between him and his family", or so she said.'

'Then she isn't a totally selfish person,' Briar suggested tentatively.

'She's quite good at sentimental claptrap. I don't suppose she'd thought through the possibility that if we were reconciled he might feel obliged to leave us a share in his estate. Cunning and logical thinking don't always go together.'

'Surely you're being a bit unfair?' she asked him as they sped by the waterfront buildings and headed for the city. 'Maybe she wanted to try and make it up to you for taking your father away.'

He gave her a sardonic glance. 'You mean she felt guilty? I don't believe that's an emotion that's ever troubled her.'

'Don't you think you might have misinterpreted her motives?' In the bitter aftermath of his parents' broken marriage, it wouldn't be surprising if his view of the woman he held responsible had been somewhat warped.

'You don't know her,' Kynan said. 'She went after my father until she had him roped and tied and standing on his head, but she'd hardly got his ring on her finger before she started casting about for diversion.'

'You mean she left him?'

'Left him? Hardly! If she'd found someone with more money—but she knew when she was on to a good thing. No, she was still married to him when he died. It infuriated her that after all that time she didn't inherit every cent he left.'

'Surely you're rather jumping to conclusions? If you never saw them after that one holiday——'

'It was enough,' Kynan said flatly. 'One thing I'll say for her, she was a pure unadulterated example of her type.'

'Her type?' Briar objected. 'If she's everything you say, she must surely be unique.'

'Hardly. I've met several who answer the description somewhat exactly. Especially since inheriting my father's fortune.' He flicked another glance at her, and Briar felt herself go hot all over.

I'm not like her! she wanted to shout at him. *I'm not!* But she sat silent and still instead, unable to refute the unspoken implication, shaken at the thought that he was comparing her with all the other greedy, needy women he'd known who were willing to sell themselves to a man for his money.

When they finally reached the house, she discovered that she'd been sitting with her hands clenched, her nails digging into her palms. She released them and said, her voice low, 'If that's so, I'd have thought the last thing you would want is marriage to another woman who...' she swallowed '...who wants money in return. Why did you...suggest it to me?'

'Do you really want to know?'

She nodded. She might not like the answer, but she felt it was important.

He said slowly, 'This way I know where we both stand. I'm under no illusions. I realise you don't like me very much at the moment, but I think we can learn to live with each other. Nothing about you grates on me, and I hope you'll tell me if the opposite is true.'

'I thought I was being paid to put up with that,' she said, out of some obscure compulsion to hit out at him.

She knew she'd managed to score a small, mean victory, but after a moment's tense silence he went on unemotionally, 'If you could try to forget the basis of our arrangement, you might find it easier to accept . . . certain things.'

'How can I forget?' she challenged him. 'Can *you*?'

'I might,' he said rather wearily, 'if you would just stop throwing it at me at every turn.'

'I'm sorry.' The apology was stiff and grudging. 'I'll try to be more the kind of fiancée you . . . have a right to expect . . .' The words *for your money* hung in the air between them. She knew he could hear them as clearly as if she'd said them aloud.

She heard him draw in a deep, steadying breath. Then he said very evenly, 'If you're spoiling for a fight, Briar, I'm just about ready to oblige you. I'd advise you to back off . . . right now!'

Her head up, adrenalin singing in her blood, she said in falsely dulcet tones, 'I thought I just did.'

'You're pushing it, lady.' He shoved open the driver's door and slammed it behind him, then came swiftly round and opened hers. 'Out,' he said.

She climbed out and faced him, her legs slightly shaky but her face serene, her mouth a little firmer than usual. She wasn't sure why she was baiting him this way, but it seemed necessary to assert herself.

'I'll see you to the door,' he said grimly, and took her arm in a grip that was surely tighter than he realised, marching her up the path. Once on the porch he released her and stood back.

Fighting an urge to rub her arm, Briar fished in the bag slung over her shoulder and found her key. Holding it in her hand, she turned to him and looked up at dark, stormy eyes and a taut mouth. 'Aren't you going to kiss me goodnight?' she asked innocently.

His eyes narrowed, and he looked at her for a long, stretched moment. 'No,' he said. He took the key from her and shoved it into the door, pushing it ajar. 'Go inside,' he said, 'before you regret that you asked.' Then he was turning to descend the shallow steps and striding away down the path.

Briar fumbled the key out of the lock and stepped into the lighted hallway.

Laura came out of the sitting-room. 'Oh, I thought you might invite Kynan in. How did your day go? Are you all right?' She looked curiously at Briar's face. 'You haven't had a row, have you?'

'No,' she said. Kynan had told her he was ready to oblige her if she wanted one. But he had more self-control than she, obviously. It was no thanks to her that they'd avoided it. She wondered why he bothered. He could have brought her to heel quite easily by reminding her how much she owed him. Literally. And that, of course, was why she'd been goading him, because it was one way of retaining some self-respect in a humiliating situation.

'How's Dad?' she asked.

'Getting better all the time.' Laura's face softened. 'Poor old dear, he's a fighter, your father.'

'You're fond of him, aren't you?' Briar asked.

Laura seemed astonished. 'Of course I am. I love Xavier.'

Briar looked at her and decided she truly meant it. She asked curiously, 'Did you always? When you married him?'

Laura said, 'That's . . . rather more complicated. Why are you asking me this now? Feeling a bit uncertain, are you?'

'How did you guess?'

'There are different kinds of loving,' Laura said. 'Probably as many different kinds as there are lovers. For some it's all sparks and fire in the beginning, and it mellows with time. And for others, it's a growing thing that starts small and becomes brighter and deeper over the years. One isn't better or worse than the other.'

Xavier's voice called, 'Laura? I need you. Was that Briar coming in?'

Laura said, 'Are you coming to have a nightcap with us?'

Briar shook her head. 'I'm going straight to bed.'

Laura had never, even in the early days of their marriage, let her feel in any way shut out. But it occurred to Briar that her father and stepmother might have valued a little more private time together. Maybe she'd stayed too long in the family home, thinking she was needed.

Maybe she'd never been as indispensable as she'd thought.

CHAPTER EIGHT

PREDICTABLY, Laura was in a flap on Briar's wedding-day. She panicked when the flowers were delivered a quarter of an hour late, kept running down to the kitchen to give last-minute instructions to the caterers, spent ten minutes feverishly hunting for her new shoes which she'd carefully laid out with her new dress the night before, and flew into Briar's room several times to ask, 'Did you remember to...?' or 'Shouldn't we have...?'

Briar was so busy calming her stepmother and patiently reassuring her that everything vital had been or would be done that she had no time to be nervous herself.

There was a moment after she slipped the white, lacy dress over her head and saw herself in the mirror when a tremor of apprehension ran through her and her eyes went dark and huge. She turned away from the disturbing image and fumbled for the short veil with its crown of tiny interwoven flowers. Surprisingly, Kynan had said that he wanted her to dress as a traditional bride, even though they'd agreed it was to be a modest affair with no bridal attendants.

Laura came in, wearing a designer gown in a soft honey colour. 'Let me do that for you,' she offered.

She fixed the head-dress and adjusted a few curling tendrils of hair, then stepped back, and her eyes shimmered with tears. 'Oh, darling, you do look beautiful. Your mother would have been so proud of you!'

Briar felt answering tears prickling behind her own eyes. Around her throat she was wearing a wrought gold star set with a single blue sapphire, which her mother had worn on her own wedding-day. Xavier had given it to Briar last night, saying gruffly, 'You...might...want to wear this. You...do...know...what you're...doing, don't you, Briar?'

It was the only, oblique indication he'd given that he had any idea what lay behind her marriage to Kynan Roth. She looked into his eyes, seeing concern and unhappiness, and said, 'Yes, I do know what I'm doing.'

'It's...not too late...to change...your mind,' he said painfully.

Briar's gaze didn't waver. 'I don't want to change my mind, Dad. I'll be all right. Kynan is ... he'll look after me very well.'

It was true, in material terms at least. He'd made more than adequate financial provision for her and her family. And he was no monster. She was sure he meant to exert every effort to ensure the stability of their marriage. It was no aim of his to make her miserable. And she had every intention of keeping her part of the bargain.

Beginning, she told herself with an access of cynicism as she checked in the mirror again while Laura hovered beside her, with presenting the package duly wrapped as ordered.

Stop it, she admonished herself. You went into this with your eyes open. With goodwill on both sides, it can work. We'll make it work. Kynan and I.

She walked down the aisle at her father's side, unobtrusively supporting him. Laura moved to help Xavier into a seat when his part was done. And Briar for the first time looked at Kynan, a tall, commanding presence at her side.

His eyes searched hers with a wordless question in them. She looked back resolutely and tried to smile.

Then the minister began intoning the words of the service, and she concentrated on giving her responses in a clear, steady voice.

When it was over they posed for photographs on the church steps and again in the grounds outside, where a small round lawn shaded by willows and planted with hebe and pink manuka made a pleasant backdrop. Then they drove back to the house, where the thirty or so guests had been invited to gather.

Laura had found a new ally in Kynan's mother, who soon had the situation assessed and became an unobtrusive helper. Briar saw Laura gradually relax and begin to look as though she was enjoying herself.

'They might be old friends,' Kynan commented, watching the two women chatting over glasses of champagne. His voice held a hint of surprise.

'Laura gets on with everyone,' Briar told him.

He glanced at her curiously. 'You really think a lot of her, don't you?' He looked again at Laura as though trying to fathom what lay beneath the prettily perfect surface, and then at Xavier, seated beside his wife.

'Don't be too quick to judge,' she said to him.

He smiled down at her. 'Reforming me already?'

'I wouldn't attempt to.'

'Why not? It's a wife's role, isn't it?'

He used the word easily. Wife, she thought. I'm his wife now, to have and to hold... from this day forward. She was suddenly shaken by the enormity of what she'd done, altering her entire life. The chattering people gathered about the buffet table seemed to recede into some dreamland, leaving her isolated with the dark stranger at her side.

'What is it?' Kynan's hand was on her arm, his fingers warm and strong. 'You need something to eat,' he diagnosed. 'Have you been drinking champagne on an empty stomach?'

She had, more or less. The tea and toast she'd swallowed for breakfast was a long time ago.

He got her a piece of chicken and some salad and made her eat it. Later the two-tier wedding cake Laura had ordered was cut to the accompaniment of cheers and good wishes. Then Kynan took Briar's arm as they circulated among the guests, thanking them for coming and for the gifts displayed in the next room.

When it was time for Briar to change, Laura went upstairs with her. Briar got into a skirt and a short-sleeved flowered blouse while Laura carefully hung up the beautiful white dress.

'I hope Kynan's taking you somewhere nice,' she said. 'But of course he will. He must know all the places...'

'We're going to stay at a holiday house belonging to a friend of his, up north on the Hokianga. He said we could go to Australia or the Cook Islands if I liked, or Hawaii. But... I liked the sound of this place.'

She hadn't wanted to spend their honeymoon at some resort where they would be under the eyes of other people. And she'd had a childish desire to stay as close to home as possible. The idea of flying to another country alone with Kynan had filled her with a stupid, inexplicable panic.

Kynan had looked pleased when she opted for the Hokianga. 'I hope you'll like it,' he said. 'I stayed there once before, when I felt in need of a break from business. It's a peaceful place, near Opononi. Ever been there?'

She hadn't, but at her first sight of the place she fell in love. The car came over a hill and she saw a glassy expanse of shimmering sea, with huge rolling hillocks of white sand rising on the other side, sand and sea glowing with the delicate pink of the dying sun that had just slipped beneath the horizon.

She caught a glimpse of a small town on the nearer shore, below a serried hillside where thick green bush almost hid the occasional house roof. Then Kynan turned the car off the main road and they wound uphill along a rough road cut between kanuka and tree ferns, eventually to arrive at a barred wooden gate.

'I'll open it.' Briar scrambled out and let the car drive through, but when he stopped it to wait for her as she closed the gate, she waved him on. She could see the house now, a low building, constructed of timber that had been allowed to weather to a soft grey, and snuggled into the hillside.

Kynan drove into a garage beside the house, then handed her a key as she joined him. 'That's the back door. I'll get the luggage.'

By the time he brought it in she had found the front room. A wall of full-length windows slid open to a broad wooden deck overhanging a slope covered in lacy umbrella-shaped ponga, polished taupata, palest pink manuka and its taller, skinnier cousin, the white-flowered kanuka. She was staring mesmerised at the glorious view of the harbour, with a long white moving line where the ocean broke against the sand bar at its entrance. Beyond the bar the limitless Pacific stretched away to a distant, rapidly dimming horizon.

When she heard his footsteps behind her, she looked around briefly and then returned her attention to the vista before them.

'Like it?' he asked, coming to stand beside her, his hands resting on the wooden rail beside hers.

'It's magnificent,' she said. 'Breathtaking.'

They stood in silence while the last of the daylight faded into dusk, the water turned to a metallic indigo and the sandhills assumed a ghostly air. Then Kynan said, 'I've put our things in the bedroom. There's a hotel in the town that does a decent meal. We could go and have dinner there if you like.'

'I'm not very hungry, but if that's what *you'd* like, I suppose they could fix me a salad . . .'

'I could fix you a salad here, if you like. We've got the ingredients.' They'd stopped at a wayside store and bought milk and other supplies.

'You?'

'I'm not totally useless in the kitchen,' Kynan said mildly. 'A salad I can manage.'

'What about you? Shall I do you some chops?'

'If you like. A couple of chops sounds good. Sure you don't want one?'

In the end she had one, while he ate two. She'd set the small table on the deck. The light spilling out from the open door attracted a few moths inside. Kynan uncorked a bottle of wine, and Briar said, 'Where did that come from? We didn't buy wine.'

'There's a supply in one of the cupboards. I'll replenish it before we leave.'

When they'd finished the bottle he opened another, declining her offer of coffee, seeming content to sit and finish the wine, savouring it and the silence around them, broken only by the occasional whirr of a passing moth or huhu beetle, and the distant boom of the waves breaking on the bar.

'We should turn out the light,' Briar said, 'so the moths will fly outside again.'

Kynan got up and went inside to do it, then returned, a looming figure in the doorway. Briar scraped back her chair and went over to the railing, staring out into the darkness where the sea was invisible now, except for a spasmodic glint here and there as the faint starlight caught a rising wavelet. Even at this distance she could smell the fresh saltiness of it, mingling with the wood-spice scent of manuka.

Kynan rejoined her and she said, 'I'll do the dishes.'

'Give the moths a chance to leave, first,' he suggested. 'Anyway, the dishes can wait till morning.'

She supposed they could. He moved beside her and she hastily shifted from the rail. 'I haven't unpacked yet.'

As she made to walk away, he caught her arm and turned her to face him. 'Are you nervous, Briar?'

She relaxed suddenly, giving a rueful laugh. 'Yes,' she confessed.

'Don't be. I promise I won't force anything. You must be tired. If you'd rather, I'll sleep in the other room tonight.'

'Thank you,' she said. That was incredibly generous of him, but she knew she couldn't expect him to keep his distance forever. Celibacy was no part of their bargain. 'There's no need for that,' she told him, determined to be sensible. 'Give me fifteen minutes to unpack and have a shower.'

She was coming out of the bathroom when he entered the bedroom. She had put on the silk-and-lace nightgown that she'd chosen for this night, with a filmy matching négligé, the most bridal thing she'd been able to find, thinking it would please him.

If the look in his eyes was anything to judge by, she'd been right. He stood just inside the door and closed it behind him, his gaze feasting on her so blatantly that she felt as though one of the moths from outside had invaded the pit of her stomach.

She put up her hands to remove the two combs she'd used to pin her hair out of the way in the shower, and saw him watching the lift of her breasts as she did so.

She flushed, standing with the combs in her hands until he came over to her and took them from her, his eyes never leaving hers. He half turned to toss the combs on to the bed nearby, and then he raised a hand and fingered a damp tendril of hair that had fallen on her forehead, lightly touched her hot cheek, and lifted her face with a hand under her chin. 'Do you know,' he whispered, his lips sensitising the skin of her temple, 'what a gloriously beautiful creature,' his breath feathered her cheek, 'you are?' And his mouth hovered over hers before closing on it with almost reverent gentleness.

She didn't know it, and she didn't believe it, but at this moment he seemed to be convinced it was so, and her body warmed to his admiration, responding to the seduction of his mouth without her conscious consent.

The kiss was long and sweet and she stood without moving until he raised his head and looked down at her, a slow fire in his eyes. His hands dropped to her shoulders, and he eased the flimsy négligé down her arms, tugging at the bow that held the waist, letting the garment fall at her feet.

Briar caught her breath, and he pushed aside the thin ribbon over her shoulder, and as the front of the gown slipped a few inches he bent his head and pressed a kiss on the exposed upper curve of her breast. Then he straightened and said huskily, 'Get into bed. I'll be right with you.' And went into the bathroom, closing the door.

With shaking fingers she picked up the négligé from the floor and placed it at the end of the bed, dropped the combs on to the dressing table, and ran a brush quickly over her hair.

She turned out the centre light, leaving a bedside lamp burning, then stripped back the cover and climbed in between cool linen sheets, closing her eyes and trying to breathe normally.

Kynan opened the bathroom door and she made herself look at him. His hair was damp and he wore nothing but a towel about his waist. His skin was lightly tanned, and with his broad shoulders and deep chest she thought he looked wonderful.

He went to the sliding glass door that opened to the deck, and threw back the curtains she had drawn against the night, then slid back the door, allowing the cool night air into the room. 'Do you mind?' He turned to her.

Briar shook her head. 'But the moths...' She looked at the bedside light.

He came over and to her relief switched it off before climbing in beside her. Outside the moon had risen, and the room was bathed in its white, cold light. 'Moonlight's nicer,' Kynan said.

He propped himself on one elbow and gazed at her, toying with her hair. 'There's nothing to be frightened of,' he told her. 'Is this your first time, Briar?'

'Yes.' She was relieved that he'd asked her. She hadn't known how to tell him.

His fingers stilled and for several long seconds there was silence. Then he said gravely, 'I'm very privileged. I'll try not to hurt you, darling.'

He had never called her that in private before. It didn't mean that he loved her, of course, but it did give her courage. Tonight, at least, he was determined to be kind, and she couldn't help but be grateful. 'I know you won't,' she told him, 'if you can help it.'

He bent his head and kissed her lips coaxingly, tenderly. And as his mouth moved to her throat he said quietly, 'You must tell me if I go too fast for you.'

But he didn't. He proceeded with exquisite slowness, touching her and kissing her tenderly, almost teasingly, and then with increasing passion as her body caught fire under his hands and his mouth, and she found herself touching him in return, caressing his hair, his shoulders, his back, raising her opened mouth to his kisses, pressing her body to the burgeoning need of his.

Until he stroked back the tumbled hair from her face and looked down at her and asked huskily, 'Now, Briar? Are you ready for me?'

And she moaned longingly, 'Yes, now! Please, now!' And felt him glide into her, and gasped.

'Are you hurting?' he asked urgently. 'I'm sorry, sweetheart. I——'

'No!' she said. 'No, it's all right. It's just . . . strange.'

It was slightly painful, and very strange, but she didn't want him to leave her. She held him to her while her body adjusted to the unaccustomed invasion and began to respond again. He kissed her brow, and she lifted her lips to him and took his seeking tongue in her mouth, heard him groan with pleasure that brought an answering dart of excitement deep inside her, felt him moving rhythmically within her and she matched him, locked together man and woman, woman and man indivisible, part of each other in the ancient, dark and secret dance of love.

The distant roar of the sea seemed to invade the room while she rode the hot black waves that tossed her higher and higher, and the darkness sharded around them and sent her spinning into an unknown dimension of ecstasy that she had never experienced or imagined.

'Briar? Briar! Are you all right?'

She was in the grip of an enormous lethargy. 'Mmm,' she murmured. 'That was...wonderful. I never knew...' Her voice trailed off. Dimly she was aware that Kynan held her cradled still in his arms, her head resting against his bare shoulder.

'I'm glad you enjoyed it. That doesn't always happen the first time. You frightened me. I thought you'd fainted.'

Perhaps she had, briefly. It was all a bit over-whelming. She wanted to sleep forever, preferably here, like this, in his arms.

But Kynan... She stirred and said drowsily, 'What about you?' She had no experience. Maybe she'd disappointed him. 'Did you...like it?'

She felt his chest shake with silent laughter. 'Oh, yes,' he said definitely. 'I certainly did, once I was sure I hadn't hurt you.'

'Good,' she said. 'I'm glad. D'you mind...if I go to sleep now?' But she never heard his reply.

Next day they visited the town, and the beach. They admired the statue of Opo, the dolphin who had made the sleepy seaside village famous in the fifties by swimming into the bay and spending the summer frolicking with tourists and the local children, before mysteriously dying.

They had lunch at one of the hotels and passed the afternoon lazing on the warm sand, walking around the rocks at low tide and, when it got too hot, going into the clear blue sea for a dip.

As they emerged side by side from the water, Kynan caught at Briar's hand and bent his wet head and kissed her lips. The kiss tasted salty and cold, but even that fleeting touch brought a quick heat to her body. She gave him a shaky smile and continued walking to where their clothes lay in a little heap beside their towels on the hot dry sand.

Kynan picked up her towel, shaking sand from it before turning to dry her dripping hair for her, gently rubbing. He draped the towel over her shoulders, still holding it, and said softly, 'I want to make love to you again. Do you mind if we go back to the house?'

Briar swallowed, and shook her head. 'No.'

'No, you don't want to? Or no, you don't mind?'

'I...don't mind.' She wanted to make love to him, too. But she wasn't quite bold enough to tell him so.

He scooped up his own towel and tucked it about his waist. 'Don't get dressed,' he said, and shoved her clothes into a bundle with his own, under one arm. 'Come on, let's go.'

It was less than a five-minute journey to the house but it seemed interminable. Small shivers of anticipation coursed through her all the way there, and they were scarcely inside the door before Kynan wrapped her in his arms and she wound hers about him, meeting his kiss with eagerly parted lips.

When he broke away from her it was only to feather more kisses down her tautened throat to the warm skin left bare by the low cut of her swimsuit.

'I'm still wet,' she said.

'We both are.' He licked salty droplets of water from between her breasts, and she shuddered with delight. 'Are you cold?' He lifted his head, his eyes glittery with desire.

'No,' she said. 'Not cold at all.'

He grinned at her and swung her into his arms, carrying her the short distance to the bedroom. He placed her on her feet beside the bed and said, 'Turn around.'

She turned her back to him and he unhooked the swimsuit at the neck, and then his hands were pushing the wet material over her hips, smoothing all the way down her legs. She stepped out of the suit and felt his hands gliding up again, and the brief touch of his lips at the back of her knees, then her thighs, on the swell of her behind as his hands reached her hips. Now his tongue was in the small of her back, tracing a line up her spine to her nape, and his hands explored her midriff and then cupped her breasts as he straightened and pulled her against him. 'You taste great, salted,' he murmured, his lips teasing her ear.

Briar tipped her head back, her eyes closed, a smile on her mouth. He bent and captured it with his own mouth, his lips moving erotically on hers as he turned her in his arms, one hand playing with her breast, sending tingles of sensation through her, while the other held her firmly, her body curving into his.

He stopped kissing her long enough to fumble the covers back from the bed and impatiently strip off his towel and bathing shorts. Briar gave a choking little laugh. 'No wonder you didn't dare stay on the beach!'

'That's what you do to me.' He grinned and took her in his arms, bringing her with him down on the bed.

Briar stretched luxuriously, filled with satisfaction and well-being. Beside her, Kynan was lying on one elbow, lazily surveying her as he wound a tendril of her hair about his fingers. 'How do you get hair this colour?' he asked her.

Briar smiled. 'Out of a bottle,' she told him.

'Really? What colour is it naturally, then?'

'Oh, fairish. The rinse gives it some life. It's not an actual dye. Do you feel cheated?' she asked him lightly. 'That you didn't get what you——'

She saw the rigidity in his face, and stopped there.

'No,' he said, but his voice had a harsh undertone now. 'I don't feel cheated. You've given me full value so far.'

He rolled away from her and got up, walking to the bathroom. As he reached the door, she said, 'Kynan——'

With his hand resting on the door-frame, he turned his head. 'Yes?'

Tightly, she said, 'That wasn't what I was going to say.'

'No? It was what you meant, though, wasn't it?' He went into the bathroom and closed the door before she could repeat her denial, and she heard the drum and hiss of the shower as he turned it on.

She sat up, dismayed and chilled. The sheets felt gritty with sand. Her wet bathing suit and Kynan's swimming-shorts lay on the mat beside the bed. She threw back the sheets and got up, grabbing a towelling robe, knotting the belt angrily about her waist. Picking up the swim-suits, she realised the mat underneath was damp, and hauled it out to the deck to sling it over the rail to dry. She returned to the bedroom, stripped the bed and shook out the sand on the deck, then took the sheets to the small laundry off the garage to wash them.

When she returned to the bedroom with fresh sheets in her arms, Kynan was there, dressed in jeans and but-toning up a white shirt.

She marched to the bed without speaking and began making it up, aware that he had turned and was watching her. When he appeared at the other side of the bed, tucking in the sheets, she said stiffly, 'It's all right. I can do it.'

'Stop sulking,' he advised her.

Briar straightened up. '*I'm* not sulking!'

His brows rose. 'Are you suggesting that I am?'

'I'm suggesting that you started this by jumping to conclusions. Something you seem to do rather often.'

He looked at her thoughtfully. 'What *were* you going to say?'

'I can't remember, exactly! I was *teasing*!' she said, to her horror feeling tears well in her eyes. 'I'd almost forgotten...why you married me,' she finished, and dashed a hand over her eyes.

'Briar!' He came swiftly round the bed and his arms went about her, holding her close.

'Don't!' she choked, trying to shove him off, but he wouldn't let her.

His lips were on her hair. 'I've been clumsy and stupid.'

'Yes, you have!' She thumped a fist against his chest, sniffing. 'And unfair!'

'And unfair,' he agreed. He tipped her head with his hand and kissed the tears from her cheeks, then lowered his lips to her hot mouth.

At first the kiss was comforting and gentle, but as her body relaxed, his lips began to explore and seduce, and she raised her arms to place them about his neck, and moved closer, pressing against him.

'Am I forgiven?' he murmured against her neck, sliding his mouth to her shoulder.

Breathlessly she answered, 'I don't know about that.' She feathered a finger along his cheek, and, as he lifted his head to look into her eyes, touched the hollow of his throat with her fingertip, and pushed her hand inside his shirt, enjoying the smooth warmth of his skin against her palm.

His eyes laughed into hers. 'I feel as though you've forgiven me.'

'Is that so?' She gave his shoulder a small pinch.

He winced and grinned down at her. 'Bitch.'

'Are you calling me names?' She curled her fingers and scraped her fingernails down his chest in a playful threat.

'Cat,' he said softly. 'Do you want to mark me?'

Her blood suddenly ran hot, desire coursing through it, sending heat into her cheeks, making her breasts tingle even though he hadn't touched them. 'Maybe I do,' she whispered, her eyes meeting his fearlessly, not trying to hide her emotions. With her other hand she began undoing his shirt.

He held her with his hands on her waist while she finished the task and drew back the edges of the shirt, baring his chest. With her eyes still holding his, she clawed her hands and raised them to his shoulders. 'Now——'

He gave a short laugh and grabbed at her wrists and shoved her down on the bed, looming over her as he scooped her hands above her head. 'Now, what?' he mocked her, thrusting a muscular thigh between hers. Her gown had fallen open and he said, 'Are you wearing anything under this thing?' His leg rubbed insinuatingly against hers.

'Find out,' she suggested defiantly.

'Right.' Kynan was smiling. He transferred both her wrists to one of his big hands and began tugging at the knotted belt. 'You really made a job of this,' he grumbled. 'What's it supposed to be? A chastity belt?'

Briar gave a small laugh. 'For all the good it will do me.'

He succeeded in loosening the belt, allowing the edges of the robe to part. His hand was shaping the narrowness of her waist, then skimming up to her breast, and she gasped, closing her eyes as he found the already hardened centre, and a pleased, knowing look crossed his face.

'You're so lovely,' he said, as if the words were torn from him.

Briar opened her eyes. 'Am I?' He had released her wrists and opened her robe completely, and his eyes swept over her. She felt her skin heating under the explicit, admiring gaze.

'As if you didn't know.' He was shouldering himself out of his shirt. 'Don't move,' he said, standing up and opening the snap of his jeans. 'I want to take you just like that.'

It was the nearest they came to quarrelling on their honeymoon. The other days passed in a haze of sunshine, swimming, sunbathing and lovemaking. Occasionally they talked to local people or other holidaymakers, and sometimes they ate out, but mostly they shared meals that they'd cooked together, and ate them on the deck, looking at the ever-changing water. One night they sat late over their dinner, watching the stars come out over the distant breakers on the bar, until the harbour entrance was just a recurring white line in the darkness. Then Kynan got up and went into the bedroom, returning with a duvet and blanket and two pillows which he carefully spread on the deck. 'Come here,' he said, holding out his hand. 'We've never made love outside, have we?'

She walked into his arms and lay down with him, and a long time later the stars left the sky and whirled about them as they lay naked and entwined in each other's arms.

'I can never have enough of this,' he told her. 'Of you.'

She felt the same. The more he made love to her the more she wanted him. He had woken a torrent of sexuality that she'd never suspected lay within her. Sometimes it alarmed her that he had only to look at her, to touch a finger to her cheek or brush a foot against hers to make her body instantly become alive with yearning to possess him again.

She thought she was falling in love with him, but he was her first and only lover. How could she know if these incredible, bewildering emotions were love, or a simple animal response to her first sexual experiences? And there was no doubt that Kynan knew exactly how to arouse her to a fever pitch. She tried not to think about where he'd learned to do that, how many other women he'd brought to the same wanton craving with the same expert tuition.

CHAPTER NINE

IF THERE was one cloud on Briar's horizon in the two weeks they spent in the little house on the Hokianga, it was the slight restraint she felt that warned her not to provoke another misunderstanding by a careless remark. She enjoyed the long, lazy days and the passion-filled nights, but never totally relaxed, reminding herself to think before she spoke.

'We haven't been to the forest,' she said to Kynan on the day before they were due to leave.

They'd talked about it, putting it off, answering the call of the beach and the surf and the distant sandhills, or the more insistent call of their bodies and the bed that they had shared so often, now.

'OK,' Kynan said. 'Today, Waipoua.'

It wasn't far to the last remnant of a kauri forest that had once covered hundreds of square miles before the settlers came from Europe and discovered the strong, beautifully grained and borer-resistant wood.

Interspersed with the colossal kauri were smaller cabbage trees and kanuka, and graceful, drooping rimu, and of course an enormous variety of ferns—from shaggy-trunked, spreading giants with tightly curled fronds at their hearts, right down to miniatures nestling among the roots of the trees.

Kynan parked the car at the head of the walkway leading to Tane Mahuta, the Father of the Forest. He took Briar's hand as they traversed the path, the fallen leaves absorbing their footsteps. Here the sun didn't penetrate the thick green cover overhead, and beads of moisture lay undisturbed on the exquisite velvety mosses that coated fallen trunks and twisting root systems alongside the path.

The pathway wound into the trees and then turned back, giving the best view of the giant kauri, its massive bulk rising bare and grey from the ground to the enormous crown where the short, tufted branches burst into the sunlight above everything else, each branch equalling a well-grown tree.

'Impressive, isn't he?' Kynan murmured as they went closer and climbed on to the decking that allowed visitors to inspect the tree without disturbing the surprisingly delicate roots.

'Oh, yes.' Briar found herself whispering in the face of such silent magnificence. She tipped back her head to survey the tree's full height. 'Amazing.' She speculated with awe on the tiny sapling of thousands of years before, now fully mature and looking set to continue standing there for a thousand or so more.

When they had read the signs giving statistics of girth, height and age, they left the platform to return to the circular path making its way back to the road, and Kynan laced his fingers into hers.

Briar skirted a puddle and caught her foot in a trailing ground plant with tiny leaves and wire-tough stems. As she stumbled, Kynan's arm whipped about her, and she clutched at his shoulder.

He didn't release her immediately, smiling at her with his eyes kindling into desire. His head came down, and his mouth met hers, clung, urgently opened her lips to him. They swayed in an embrace that neither wanted to break, until the sound of voices broke them apart and Kynan, his arm still firm at her waist, moved her aside to make way for a family party coming down from the road.

He kept his arm about her until they reached the car, and when they had got in he said, 'Do you want to go on, or back to the house?'

'Back,' she said huskily, and he slanted her a smile and started the car, turning it to face the way they had come.

Five minutes after their arrival they were in bed.

Later they got up and went down to the beach for a last stroll along the white sand, and dinner at the hotel. And that night they made love again, savouring every exquisite moment, prolonging the anticipation until they could wait no longer for each other, reaching the heights together and lying in each other's arms for ages bathed in the blissful aftermath.

Lingering on the deck next morning over a late breakfast before leaving the Hokianga, Briar thought that she would never again experience such near-perfect happiness.

Kynan returned to his office in the morning, and that afternoon she visited her father and Laura.

'You look blooming!' Laura greeted her. 'Marriage obviously agrees with you.'

Her father, too, seemed to relax after a sharp glance at her as she kissed his cheek. 'He's...looking after...you all right, then,' he said, apparently a statement rather than a question. His speech had improved markedly in the short time she'd been away.

'Yes,' Briar said. And that was the end of it.

She left in plenty of time to buy some ingredients for a very special dinner, and when Kynan arrived home she was dressed in a pretty frock and setting the table with wedding-gift china and crystal, while a bottle of wine stood chilling in the refrigerator.

He greeted her with a lingering kiss and murmured into her hair, 'You look good enough to eat.'

'I've something better,' she said. 'It'll be ready in fifteen minutes.'

'I'll have a shower first,' he said. 'Care to join me?'

If she did, they'd never get to eat her special dinner, not until much later when it would be spoiled. She slipped out of his arms. 'I'm busy in the kitchen. You wouldn't want your dinner burning up, would you?'

'Why not? I am.'

She laughed and left him standing in the hall.

After two days of settling in, making room for her clothes in Kynan's wardrobe and drawers, hanging a couple of her favourite pictures, and adding some books and records to his collections, Briar too was ready to return to work. She phoned Pat and said, 'I'll be in tomorrow.'

'Good,' he replied. 'I've missed you.'

He greeted her with a hug and stood back, looking at her. 'My, my. Getting married has certainly done something for you!'

She flushed, and laughed. 'I'm sure you're imagining things.'

'Oh, yeah?' Pat turned to open a box of newly arrived stock. 'I hope you and Kynan aren't planning to start a family right away. I'd hate to lose you permanently.'

'You'd find someone else,' she said. 'And if we do, I'll give you plenty of notice.'

He looked at her with sharp enquiry.

Briar shook her head. 'Not yet,' she assured him.

But Kynan did want a family, she reminded herself. It was part of the reason he'd married her. The thought of having his child was both scary and exciting.

She invited Kynan's mother and Xavier and Laura to come to dinner. She thought the evening was a success, and afterwards said so as she changed into her nightdress while Kynan lay on the bed, wearing only pyjama trousers, and idly watched her.

'Yes,' he agreed. 'Your father seems somewhat improved.'

'He is.' She came to join him, pulling up the sheet over them both. 'I'm sure he's much better since he's been able to stop worrying about his finances.' She leaned over, her hand on his chest, and said, 'And that's due to you.' Her lips touched his cheek. She added huskily, 'I can't thank you enough, Kynan.'

He sat up, his hands gripping her shoulders. 'Yes, you can,' he said. 'And you know exactly how to, don't you?'

Shocked, she blinked at him, her cheeks paling. 'I . . . try,' she said.

It was the wrong thing to say. His eyes narrowed, his lips going tight. 'Well, don't tell me it's a hardship,' he said, and bore her back against the pillows with a long, intensely sexual kiss.

There was a deliberation about his lovemaking that night that left her feeling emotionally bruised. It wasn't that she hadn't responded. She had, but even as she writhed in his arms and clutched at him in the culmination of passion and felt his answering shudder, she was aware that he was somehow distanced from what they were experiencing, and was watching both himself and her with cynical detachment.

*   *   *

The following Saturday they'd been invited to visit Briar's parents for lunch.

After the dishes were cleared, Laura asked Briar to come into the garden, on the pretext of showing her a new azalea she'd bought.

Fingering the petals of a white bush rose nearby, Laura said, 'Briar, your father and I have decided to sell this house.'

'Sell it?' Briar repeated in astonishment.

'I know it was your home, and you must be attached to it, but you're married now with a home of your own.' There was a hint of pleading in Laura's voice. 'And Xavier and I could do with something smaller.'

'I thought you loved this place,' Briar told her, bewildered. 'You've always cherished it so.'

Laura gave her an odd little smile. 'I appreciate its beauty and I've felt a duty to preserve it. I hope whoever buys it will care for it, but... actually I never really felt it was mine. And after all these years, I'd like a place that's truly my own.'

Briar found herself rearranging a number of things she'd always taken for granted. It wasn't, these days, a new experience. 'Did you ever tell Dad how you felt?'

Laura shook her head. 'Don't get me wrong, Briar. I don't hate living here. It's a beautiful house, and your mother did a wonderful job with it.'

'You've left it pretty much as you found it, haven't you?' Briar asked.

'I thought it was important for you that we didn't disrupt your life when I married your father, and I didn't like to change things too much.'

'Only it might have made you feel that you belonged here if you had,' Briar guessed.

'Maybe. After a while I mentioned to Xavier that I'd like to replace some of the furnishings, but he didn't see the point. And I realised that no matter what I did, it would always be more your mother's house than mine. I knew I could never live up to her. She must have been a pretty special person.'

'I suppose she was,' Briar said, remembering an energetic, capable and carelessly affectionate woman who always seemed to have a list of some sort in her hand, or a telephone pressed to her ear. 'But so are you.'

Laura looked mildly astonished. 'That's awfully sweet of you. No—I'm very ordinary. And not clever, or anything. Not like Xavier and his . . . friends. That's why it's always been an ordeal for me organising your father's business entertaining. We don't need to do that any more, now he's decided to be sensible and retire. In a smaller house—a flat, maybe—I'll have more time to spend with him. And he . . . he needs me, now.'

'He always did.'

Laura smiled and shook her head again. 'You did.'

'Is that . . . why you married him?' Briar asked slowly. Laura, with her penchant for undervaluing herself, was perhaps happiest when she felt needed. Was it meeting Briar, twelve years old and missing her mother, that had swayed a pretty young widow into a second marriage with a much older man?

But Laura said, 'No. I needed him. He was my knight in shining armour.'

As Briar blinked, Laura laughed gently. 'I know it's difficult for you to see your father in that role. But that's how he seemed to me. My first husband—well, we were young and of course we were madly in love. It was lovely, except that we didn't have a lot of money and there were no children. We kept putting that off, but it would have been nice, though in the end I suppose it was for the best. We weren't to know that Arnie would be killed in a car accident when he was only thirty-one.' She lifted a finger and wiped away a tear. 'We'd had our ups and downs—there was even another woman, once. It took a long time for me to forgive him for that, but we weathered it in the end. It wasn't a bad marriage. And then suddenly, in the blink of an eye, it was over.'

'That must have been awful.'

'Yes, it was. When I met your father he was one of the few people who understood just how awful it was. He'd been through the same thing. Xavier's never been one to show his feelings much, but he was kind to me, and I suppose he was lonely, too. He seemed very solid and he gave me a feeling of security that was the one thing I'd never had with Arnie. Of course we weren't in love the way I had been at eighteen. But we do love each other, Briar. He's a good husband. And you were a bonus.' She put out a hand and touched Briar's arm. 'I'd read up on all the problems of step-relationships, and was prepared for the worst. But you were such a lovely little girl. I could hardly believe my luck.' She laughed.

'Neither could I.' Briar grinned back at her. 'I thought I was the lucky one.' Laura had hung back from emotional intimacy at first in her anxiety not to do the wrong thing, never expecting anything that her new stepdaughter was not prepared to give. It meant Briar had made all the first moves, which Laura welcomed with warmth and open arms. Laura's capacity for loving was generous, and she'd been boundlessly willing to put aside any other consideration when Briar needed her. After a time Briar had felt closer to her than she could recall ever being to her natural mother.

'Laura?' Kynan's voice called. 'You're wanted on the phone.'

As Laura hurried to answer it, Kynan came towards Briar, slipping an arm about her shoulder as they walked more slowly back to the house.

The episode after the dinner party had left her with a lingering distaste, a kind of shame, and she'd manufactured several excuses not to make love with him since. She found herself stiffening involuntarily under his casual caress, and forced herself to stay within the circle of his arm, hoping he wouldn't notice her reluctance.

On the way home she asked him, 'Did Dad say anything to you about selling the house?'

'No. What makes you think...?'

'Laura told me they plan to move somewhere smaller. It'll be easier for her.'

'You said she loved the place.'

'I know I did, but...it seems I was wrong. She was only worried that I'd be upset if they disposed of it.'

And after a while he said, 'Would you like me to buy it?'

Briar turned in her seat. '*Would* you?' Then she said, 'No, you've done enough already.'

He said, 'It would be a good home for a family.'

A family. So far there was no sign of their starting one, but it was early days yet.

'I...don't know,' she said. The house held both happy memories and sad ones. She couldn't help a tug of regret that it might pass into the hands of strangers. 'Whatever you like.'

His brows creased, and he shot her a slightly impatient look. 'Think about it. I could make your father an offer.'

'I told you,' she said, 'it's up to you.' She owed him so much already, she couldn't ask him to do this at her sentimental whim.

Briar knew she would be unable to maintain the excuses for much longer. When Kynan took her in his arms that night she reminded herself that she had no right to refuse him. Tentatively she slid her own arms about his neck and began to kiss him back.

But for the first time she failed to reach a climax, lying passive and unresisting while finally Kynan crested the wave alone.

'I'm sorry,' he said afterwards as she moved away from him. 'What did I do wrong?'

'Nothing,' Briar answered remotely. 'It isn't you, it's me.'

'So, what's the matter?'

Nothing that hadn't been the matter before, if she were honest. Not for the first time she told herself that she'd known what she was in for when she married him. Nothing had changed.

'I...can't explain,' she said. 'I'm tired. Can I go to sleep now?'

For a moment there was silence. Then he said, 'Of course. You don't need to ask my permission.'

Kynan brought some business acquaintances home for dinner at short notice, and, even though she had to leave the boutique early and do some last-minute shopping before rushing home to cook, he seemed pleased with the result. After the guests had gone he poured the last of a bottle of sparkling wine into two glasses and told her so, toasting her with his eyes. 'That seemed highly successful. You did a great job.'

'It's one of the things you married me for, after all,' she told him lightly, biting her lip immediately afterwards on the remark. She'd already drunk quite a lot of wine over dinner, otherwise she might have remembered to guard her tongue.

There was a strained silence before Kynan said evenly, 'That's right, so it was. It wasn't the only thing, however. Come here, Briar,' he added softly, putting down the drink he'd barely touched.

After the smallest hesitation she obeyed, trying to ignore the loud, uneven beating of her heart. She stopped two feet from him and took a quick drink from her own glass, trying to imbibe some courage.

He stretched out a hand and took the glass from her, sipped at it himself, holding her eyes with his, and placed it beside his own. 'Closer,' he said, and took her hands with his, drawing her nearer. With only inches between them, his gaze roved over her shoulders, left bare by a slim-waisted, shoestring-strapped tangerine silk dress, and back to her face, lingering on her mouth. His hands released hers and slid up her arms, grasping her shoulders lightly. 'I bought the house,' he said. 'As soon as your father and Laura move out, we can move in...if you want.'

'Was it...a good buy,' she asked him, 'from your point of view?' It bothered her that he might have done it for her sake.

'I paid a fair price, not an exorbitant one. It's in an area where it should maintain its value, and it'll be ideal for entertaining, besides being more suitable for a family than this.'

Briar didn't know if he expected her to thank him. She felt a confusion of emotions. Her eyelids fluttered as she looked down, her gaze fixed on the shadowy

hollow of his throat, where he'd undone the top buttons
of his shirt after discarding his tie.

'Look at me,' he said.

Her eyes unwillingly rose to his. His were burning,
penetrating. She felt he was trying to get inside her soul.
'Don't you have anything to say?'

'I don't know what I'm supposed to say. What do you
want of me, Kynan?' she whispered, half afraid of him.
Her eyes were wide on his face.

His reply stunned her with its unexpectedness. 'I want
you,' he said slowly, 'to tell me that you love me.'

Her lips parted in surprise. She stared at him, her
stomach lurching, her heart beating an erratic tattoo.
She felt hot, and cold. As if she wanted to weep, or
scream with fury.

I do! she thought with unexpected, piercing clarity. I
love him. But the words wouldn't come. He wanted her
to say them, but he'd given no indication that her feelings
were reciprocated. It wasn't even clear whether he was
asking her to love him, or just to repeat an empty
formula. She didn't know what his motives were.

In the welter of emotions, anger finally won out. She
swallowed hard, forced herself not to look away, and
said, 'I won't say those words when they mean nothing.
There are some things your money won't buy.'

He blinked once, and his face went totally expressionless. Then his lips stretched in a mirthless smile.
'Fair enough,' he said. 'Then I'll just have to settle for
the substitute. They say, don't they, that actions speak
louder than words?'

His hands tightened on her shoulders, drawing her inexorably to him, and he lowered his mouth to hers in a
long, merciless kiss.

Still angry, she stood rigidly in his grasp with her hands clenched at her sides, and refused to reciprocate. Until at last he lifted his head and looked down into her defiant eyes. He gave a soft laugh that sent shivers chasing up and down her spine, and swept her up in his arms, striding to the bedroom.

He put her down by the bed and said curtly, 'Get undressed.'

'No!'

His eyebrows rose. 'It's a very lovely dress, but surely you don't intend to sleep in it?'

Feeling foolish, which didn't improve her temper, Briar turned to grab her nightgown from under the pillow and marched into the bathroom with it, slamming the door.

She undressed in there, regretting as she pulled on the nightgown that it was a filmy affair, lace-trimmed and all too revealing. She threw her undies into the laundry basket and returned to the bedroom holding the dress, going straight to the wardrobe to hang it up. By the time she turned, Kynan was taking his turn in the bathroom, and she hastily scrambled into bed.

She had her back to the door when she heard him come out and the light snapped off. The mattress depressed under his weight, and his amused voice said, 'You can't be asleep yet, so stop pretending.'

'I'm tired,' she said without turning.

His fingers stroked up her arm, and down again. 'How tired?'

'Very.'

'Why are you so angry?' he asked her. His fingers were on her back now, where the nightgown dipped provocatively. He shifted closer, and she felt his lips nuzzle her shoulder.

'I'm not angry.' Briar blinked back tears. She wasn't, any more, but there was an ache about her heart. She closed her teeth. The last thing she wanted was for Kynan to know that she was hurt.

His lips wandered to her nape, then began pressing tiny kisses down her spine. The bedclothes rustled as he pushed them aside. 'I always liked this gown.'

She'd worn it several times on their honeymoon, but never for very long. It had usually ended up in a discarded heap on the floor of the bedroom. Memories chased each other around in her mind, and her breathing quickened as Kynan's hands and mouth evoked a torrent of memories, along with more immediate sensations.

He said huskily, 'Kiss me goodnight and I'll let you go to sleep.'

She turned into his arms and kissed him, intending it to be brief and almost passionless. But the touch of his lips seduced her and they clung together wordlessly until he lowered the straps of the nightgown and began fondling her breasts. She sighed into his mouth, felt him push the gown further down, his hands gliding over her stomach, and after that she was lost.

Xavier and Laura moved into a brand new town house that Laura set about furnishing and decorating with huge enthusiasm. Xavier had improved a lot, and developed an interest in orchid-growing in the conservatory which was attached to the living area. He seemed to have mellowed considerably, and was not so inclined to be sharp with Laura. She was more serene, too, and had gained confidence. Even Kynan noticed she was doing less fluttering and fussing.

Perhaps, Briar thought, after she and Kynan had visited them one evening, Xavier's low-key but persistent fault-finding, often disguised as indulgent amusement, had been a rather pathetic and mis-aimed attempt at making himself seem clever and important, belittling Laura's talents by contrast with his own, so that she would continue to look up to him.

Kynan said, 'Laura certainly cares for your father very well. He's been remarkably fortunate.'

'You thought she married Dad for his money, didn't you?'

He gave her a sideways glance. 'The thought crossed my mind, I admit.'

'Not all women are like your father's dollybird, you know. You shouldn't let one experience sour you for good.'

A frown appeared between his brows. 'I didn't think that I had. Actually I like women.' He gave her a quizzical look.

Briar quelled a stab of unreasonable jealousy. She couldn't be unaware that he'd known other women besides herself, for heaven's sake. But he'd never given her any reason for doubt since marrying her. And for that she ought to be thankful.

'Have you decided what furniture you want to take from the flat when we move into the house?' he asked her, changing the subject.

'There isn't much that would suit it. Anything you're fond of, we'll take, of course.'

'I'm not attached to anything, except my paintings. Laura said some of the drapes and chair covers need renewing, and she thought we might want to repaper. Shall I get an interior designer to draw up a plan, or do you want to do it yourself?'

'I'd like to do it. Would you mind...if I gave Pat notice?'

'And stopped work?' He looked at her keenly. 'If you think you'll have enough to do, it's fine with me.'

'If I'm to redo the house I'll have plenty to keep me occupied,' she said. 'For a while at least.' She left unspoken the thought that by the time she'd finished that task she might have a baby, or at least the prospect of one, to occupy her.

The knowledge that she loved him was a disturbing new factor in Briar's relationship with Kynan. It made her vulnerable, and sometimes that was unsettling. She called at his office one day to ask his opinion of some wallpaper samples, and discovered that his secretary was young and attractive, and wore no wedding-ring. She found herself watching them both for signs of a more intimate relationship.

It occurred to her that Kynan had not included promises of fidelity in the terms of their pre-marriage contract, and when he phoned to say he'd be late home as some business matter had cropped up requiring urgent attention she spent the evening fighting off fantasies of him seeing another woman.

It was ridiculous and demeaning, she told herself. She wouldn't give in to such absurd suspicions. He wasn't the type to cheat on his wife, even a wife he'd married for reasons other than love.

But Kynan was an attractive man. Supposing he fell in love one day—with someone else?

It didn't bear thinking about. I'd let him go, she told herself bleakly. No, I wouldn't—I'd fight tooth and nail for him. But she knew she couldn't hold him against his will. If his happiness lay with another woman, she'd have to make the ultimate sacrifice.

If only she could become pregnant. Surely if she were having his child the balance would tip in her favour? They'd been married six months now, and still her cycle was relentlessly regular.

'Be patient,' Laura advised when she tentatively mentioned her disappointment. 'I understand, but give it time. Doesn't Kynan want you to himself for a while before you start having babies?'

'He hasn't said so,' Briar mumbled. No way could she tell Laura that having her to himself was not one of Kynan's priorities. 'You don't think there could be something wrong with me?'

'I can't think of any reason there should be anything wrong,' Laura assured her. 'But if you're worried you could get a doctor to check you over.'

The doctor found no cause for concern, suggesting just as Laura had that she be patient, but 'If nothing has happened within a year or so, we can arrange more extensive tests.' Pausing, he added, 'At that point, it might be wise for your husband to be tested, too.'

She didn't mention the visit to Kynan. Time enough when and if a second check became necessary.

Unlike Laura, she'd had no qualms about putting her own stamp on the old house. She'd tried to keep within the character of the place, but made the rooms seem more cheerful and airy with fresh, paler wallpapers and lighter-weight curtains. She cleared most of the heavy furniture out of the library and turned it into a comfortable and efficient study for Kynan, and shopped for a new lounge suite to put in the TV room, as well as completely refurbishing the master bedroom.

Surprisingly, Kynan had expressed a curiosity to see her old bedroom before she started altering it.

She stood hesitantly in the doorway as he wandered about, surveying the pink-sprigged wallpaper and rosewood dressing-table, and casting her a surprised smile as he lifted the shabby rag doll that sat on top of the bookcase.

'That's Woozy,' she said. 'I had much prettier dolls, but she's been around since I was three years old, and somehow I always loved her more than the others.'

Kynan looked down at the battered object and said gravely, 'Hi, Woozy,' before replacing the doll carefully on the bookcase. He bent and took a copy of *Tarzan of the Apes* from one of the shelves. 'I didn't know you were a Tarzan fan.'

'Isn't every twelve-year-old? Male or female. I have to admit I came to it via television, though.'

Replacing *Tarzan* and pulling out the small book next to it, he said, 'I've never read this. *Daddy-Long-Legs*. Wasn't that a film, too? What's it about?'

'It's a love story, and yes, it was a film, but I liked the book better.'

He flipped through the pages. 'Letters. Hmm. Is this twelve-year-old reading, too?'

Briar laughed. 'Yes, but I've re-read it many times since.'

'When your love-life went wrong?'

Briar shook her head. 'Not necessarily. The first time was after my mother died.' She bit her lip. She hadn't meant to let that slip. 'It was...comforting, somehow.'

'Was it?' He looked down at the cover picture of a lonely girl in old-fashioned clothes gazing out of a window. 'Shall I read it to you again?'

He looked serious, not teasing. She said, 'Do you think I need comfort?'

'I don't know. Do you?'

Briar didn't answer, because a lump in her throat prevented a reply.

'Come here.' Kynan held out his free hand. When she moved slowly forward and put hers into it, he drew her to the single bed in front of the window and pulled down the cover, propping the cushions against the rosewood bedhead. 'Sit,' he said, and when she did he swung her legs up and settled himself beside her, putting an arm about her to settle her against his shoulder. 'Now.' He opened the book. '"The first Wednesday in every month was a Perfectly Awful Day——"'

'Your turn,' he told her some time later. 'I'm getting hoarse. Besides, I don't think my voice is exactly right for reading the letters of a fifteen-year-old girl.'

'You must be bored,' Briar objected.

'I'm not in the least bored. I hope this story has a happy ending, though. I'll be very disappointed if it doesn't.'

'You'll find out,' she said, knowing he wasn't in any doubt, really.

When she turned the last page and read the final words, he said, 'Is that a tear?' and wiped her cheek with his finger.

'I always cry when I reach the end,' she confessed.

'Why? She gets her man, and he has his girl, and they live happily ever after—although there is that small admission that in the nature of things one of them must probably die before the other. Interesting in such a basically sentimental story.'

'But, as she says, they will have had their happiness together.'

'Mmm.' He took the book from her hand and dropped it on to the carpet. 'Do you know what I've been thinking for the last fifteen minutes?'

'You mean you weren't really thinking about poor Judy and how she nearly lost her dear and only love?'

He shifted and threw a leg across hers, looking down at her. 'That, too. And very moving stuff it was. But I was also thinking...' he traced the line of her cheek to her jaw '...of you sleeping in this bed, alone.' His head lowered and he put his lips to her throat, and flicked open a button and kissed her there, too. 'And that for once I'd like to share it with you,' he went on, opening some more buttons.

'It isn't a very big bed,' she said feebly. His wandering mouth was awakening shivers of pleasure wherever it touched, and his deep, quiet voice was hypnotic. When he was tender and kind like this, she could almost believe that he loved her. She moved very slightly, bringing her more intimately close to him, a subtle invitation.

'It's big enough,' Kynan said, lifting his head, his mouth hovering over hers. 'Trust me.'

CHAPTER TEN

KYNAN had been persuaded to buy tickets to a gala benefit performance of modern dance. 'Do you want a new dress?' he asked Briar. 'Use my credit card.'

'No,' she said, 'I've plenty of dresses.'

Wondering if the sharp look he slanted at her implied a criticism, she added, 'If you want me to wear something new, of course I will. Would you prefer I spent more on clothes? Or don't you like my taste?'

'What on earth are you on about?' he asked. 'Have I offended you by offering to pay for a dress?'

'Of course not. You're always very generous.' Ignoring his frown, she went on, 'But if you think I ought to show more interest in fashion——'

'I wasn't saying what you *ought* to do, merely passing a comment. You always look very...polished. I noticed it the first moment I saw you.'

'Polished?'

'It wasn't an insult. I suppose it's something you learned from your stepmother.'

'What *is* it that you have against Laura?' she demanded.

'I've got nothing against her at all.'

'Yes, you have. Every time you mention her I sense some kind of snide undercurrent.'

'You're imagining things. Why do you feel she needs protecting? Does your father bully her?'

Briar shook her head. 'Of course not—at least——'

'At least, what?'

153

She bit her lip. 'Organising parties and attending social occasions was always torture for her.'

'Really?'

'Surely you noticed how agitated she got?'

He seemed sceptical, Briar thought. He probably thought it was a pose, a way of getting attention. Trying to explain, she went on. 'I think each time she worked herself up into more of a tizz, so it got worse and worse. And Dad just got irritated. He could never understand how she felt about it. It's better now that she doesn't have to do it any more.'

'So, taking him out of the business limelight has done some good, then.'

'I suppose it has. Laura's happier, anyway.'

'Good. I'm glad for her.'

Briar looked at him in helpless irritation. She couldn't fault the words, yet there was still that slightly acid undertone to his voice.

The charity gala was a glittering occasion, the theatre reception area packed with patrons in evening dress, the lights occasionally catching a diamond sparkle or dancing off a sequined dress. Briar recognised some of the people who used to attend her father's parties, many whom she and Kynan had entertained or been entertained by since their marriage.

But she didn't recognise the woman who, winding her way through the crowd with a glass of champagne in her hand, halted before them with her brown eyes widening in surprise and said, 'Ky! Fancy seeing you here!'

Glancing up at Kynan, Briar thought he had a very odd look on his face. She wasn't sure what it meant, except that he was suddenly tense and definitely not pleased as he said, 'I might say the same, Isa.'

Isa? Briar couldn't recall anyone mentioning Isa to her. An old flame, perhaps? She looked closely at the woman. About Kynan's own age, she guessed at first. But no—rather older, though the expert make-up, flowing dark hair and a luscious if slightly overripe figure encased in form-fitting red stretch lace easily disguised the fact.

'I'm here with Nolan Cross,' she said. 'You know, the property developer?'

'I know him,' Kynan said woodenly.

'Oh, don't look so disapproving.' Her reddened lips assumed a pout. 'I'm entitled to come out of my weeds, you know.'

'Were you ever in them?' Kynan enquired, eyeing the red dress.

Isa laughed prettily, although there was a high edge to it. 'Well, you know, metaphorically speaking. Actually, Cal always hated me in black! I don't really think he'd want me wearing it in his memory. And who's your little friend?' She looked curiously at Briar.

With obvious reluctance, Kynan said, 'This is my wife.'

'Your *wife*!' the woman squealed, so that several people nearby looked around. 'Ky, you dark horse! It must have been a quiet little wedding?' Her eyes quickly skimmed over Briar's flat stomach.

'Fairly,' Kynan said, his eyes warning her. 'Eight months ago.'

Isa put her head on one side, smiling up at him. 'I'm so happy for you,' she cooed, her eyes going soft and shining. 'I wish I'd known about it, to send a present. Not that I would have expected to be invited, of course. But still...' Her sultry face took on a wistful look. 'Anyway, congratulations—both of you.' She held out a hand to Briar who took it bemusedly in hers. Isa leaned forward and kissed her cheek. 'I hope you'll be very, very happy. And you, Ky.' She went on tiptoe to kiss his unresponsive mouth, leaving a trace of lipstick and almost spilling the wine in her hand as she stepped back.

Startled, Briar detected a glitter of tears in the guileless brown eyes. Isa blinked them away. 'Don't look like that,' she said to Kynan. 'Heavens, we're almost family, after all.' She put a hand on Kynan's arm, and said to Briar, 'He's always disapproved of me, you know. Haven't you, Ky?' Turning a coquettish smile on him, she added, 'Never mind, here's to love...and marriage.' She raised her glass and took a large gulp, then laughed again and said, 'Must be off. Nolan will be wondering where I am.'

It wasn't until they had returned to the auditorium and were seated that Briar asked quietly, 'Who is Isa?'

'You don't know?' He turned to her. 'Of course, I didn't complete the introduction properly. I suppose,' he added reluctantly, 'that you'd call her my stepmother.'

That was his father's second wife? The dollybird that his sister had spoken of so bitterly? 'She must have been very young,' Briar said involuntarily.

'When they met? She was twenty-one,' Kynan said. 'And she hasn't changed a bit.'

The music began and the lights dimmed then, so that even if she'd been able to think of anything to say it wouldn't have been possible.

Kynan's mother mentioned that his birthday was coming up, and Briar invited her and Madeline and David for a surprise dinner, and then set about finding a present for him.

After discarding several ideas, and wandering in and

out of shops opening and shutting books, scrutinising paintings and prints and picking up and putting down various leather goods, she went to the boutique where she'd worked and, after being introduced to his new assistant, appealed for Pat's help.

'Something for the man who has everything, huh?' He grinned at her. 'Including you.'

'Nobody has everything,' Briar said. 'Come on, Pat—give me some ideas.'

'Got some nice tooled leather belts in the other day,' he offered helpfully. 'Or there's the Italian silk handkerchiefs—a box of six in different colours. Or... cufflinks are making a comeback. Everyone's wearing them. Lovely pair of greenstone ones set in gold, done by a woman in Hokitika. With a matching tie-tack. How does that grab you?'

He took a satin-lined box from a showcase and handed it to her. 'They're hand-crafted, not mass-produced stuff.'

'Perfect,' she said, knowing instantly that this was what she'd been searching for. The jade, cut into matching diamond shapes, was a dark, mysterious green polished to a high sheen, in a simple gold setting. The set looked understated and elegant and very expensive. 'How much?' she asked, and wrote him a cheque. It wouldn't leave much in the personal savings account she'd had before her marriage, but she didn't want to use Kynan's money to buy his present.

'Want it gift-wrapped?'

'No, I'll do it myself.' She intended to choose a card to go in with it.

'OK. What's it like being married to a high-powered type like him?' Pat asked as he put the box into a paper bag and sealed it with tape.

'Is that a rhetorical question?'

Pat leaned his elbows on the counter and studied her. 'Not necessarily. You're happy, are you?'

'Yes,' Briar answered, hoping she sounded confident, 'of course.'

'Hmm.' He regarded her with interest. 'You in a hurry?' Before she could answer, he added, 'It's only half an hour till closing. Kelly can manage alone for that short time. Come and have a drink with me?'

When she had been working here they would sometimes repair to a nearby bar and have a couple of glasses of wine before going home, a good way to unwind at the end of a particularly busy or stressful day.

'That'd be nice,' she agreed. It would be like old times, and she felt a tug of nostalgia for those days when she had been single and heartfree and not caught up in the bittersweet throes of unreciprocated love.

The bar was small and crowded, but by some miraculous chance a couple were just leaving as Briar and Pat squeezed past, looking for a seat, and he immediately thrust her into the leather banquette half-circling a minute table and said, 'What'll you have?'

She opted for a white wine, and Pat disappeared into the mass, to emerge some time later holding two glasses triumphantly aloft.

She placed her bag and the parcel containing Kynan's present on the table and took one of the glasses.

Pat raised his to her. 'Here's to happy ever after,' he intoned.

Briar smiled and sipped at the cool liquid. 'And to business,' she said. It had been one of their regular toasts. 'How is it?'

'Since you left—dismal.'

She looked at him in surprised concern.

He said, 'I've yet to see signs of the improvement in the economy they're talking about. So far I've just been keeping my head above water. I might have to sell up.'

'Oh, Pat! I'm so sorry.'

He shrugged. 'Life's a gamble. Something else will turn up. So, how's it been treating you? Honeymoon over, is it?'

'Why do you say that?' She raised her head defensively.

'I've known you for a long time. Problems?'

'Nothing major.' She bit her lip, realising that she'd just admitted her happiness was less than ideal.

Pat said, 'Remember when you held my hand and let me cry on your shoulder after I broke up with Angela? I'd always be willing to return the favour if you wanted me to.'

She smiled at him. 'I know. And if I ever need it, I'll let you know. But really...' she shook her head '...there isn't anything...'

'If you say so. Well...' He put a hand over hers, lying on the table. 'If you want me, you know where to find me.'

'Thanks, Pat. You're a pal.' She leaned across the small space between them and kissed his cheek, then freed her hand.

And Kynan's voice said, 'Hello, Briar.'

She started, and quickly swept the parcel off the table into her lap. 'Kynan! What are you doing here?'

'Having a drink with a colleague.' He didn't deflect the question back to her, but his glance between her and Pat spoke volumes. 'Good evening, Pat.'

'Hi.' Pat shifted in his seat. 'Briar and I were having a drink for old times' sake.'

'Really?' The chillingly polite voice made Briar's hackles rise. He was making her feel like a woman caught in adultery, and that was not only stupid, it was insulting.

Pat flushed, his expression becoming mulish. 'Yes, really.' His inflexion invited Kynan to make something of it.

But Kynan wasn't taking any notice of him. 'If you're ready,' he said to Briar, 'I'll take you home. Unless you have your car?'

Briar shook her head. 'No, I don't. But we were about to have another drink,' she added boldly, although their glasses were more than half full.

'I did promise her a couple,' Pat said.

'Of what?' Kynan's voice was edged with steel. After the slightest pause he added smoothly, '*I'll* get my wife's drink. White wine, is it, Briar?'

'Won't your colleague be waiting for you?' she asked.

'He just left. I was on my way out myself. Do you want that drink or not?'

'No,' she said. 'Never mind.' She gulped down the rest of her wine and gathered up her bag, stuffing the package into the pocket of her jacket as she stood up. 'Thanks for...everything, Pat. I'll be seeing you.'

He stood up. 'Sure. Take care, Briar.'

She smiled at him, and impulsively kissed his cheek again. ''Bye.'

Kynan took her arm as they left the bar, and outside he turned her with him, striding down the street.

Too proud to ask him to slow down, Briar lengthened her steps to keep up with him, quietly seething.

As he opened the door for her, she saw that his mouth was grim, his jaw tightly clenched.

He went round and unlocked the driver's door, but didn't immediately get in, and when he did slide in beside her he sat with his hands on the wheel before taking a deep, sighing breath and thrusting the key into the ignition. She had the impression that he'd been calming himself.

As he swung the car into the traffic, she said, 'It wasn't an assignation, you know.'

'Did I suggest that it was?'

'You seemed ... put out.'

He spared her a single, searing glance. 'I've no reason to be ... have I?'

'No. Pat's an old friend.'

'So you told me.'

'Then you don't object to me having a drink with him?'

He said rather silkily, 'Did you perhaps hope that I would object?'

'*No*! I didn't know you were going to come into that bar, did I?'

'Precisely.'

'What does that mean, exactly?' she demanded, twisting in her seat.

He said, slowing for a traffic-light before turning off the busy main road, 'You have every right to see your old friends, Briar. I have not raised any objection. So there's no reason for you to be upset. Is there?'

'I'm not upset.' He was right, yet she felt nettled as much by his apparently reasonable attitude now as by his high-handedness in the bar. For a few minutes she'd wondered if he was jealous. However unfounded, jealousy at least would indicate that he had some strong feelings about her. Now it seemed she'd imagined the whole thing.

He said, as if only mildly interested, 'Been shopping?'

'Yes.'

'So... did you buy yourself something pretty?'

'No.' She wasn't in the mood to tell him she'd bought him a birthday present. 'It wasn't that kind of shopping.'

They lapsed into silence, and Briar unhappily stared out of the window at a tree-lined street of gracious colonial homes with lace curtains at the windows and wide verandas.

As they neared home she said, 'Pat thinks he may have to sell the boutique. He's having trouble keeping it going.'

Kynan changed gears and drove into their street. 'Does he think you might get me to bail him out?'

'What?' She turned to stare at him.

He slowed and swung the car into the driveway, pressing a button on the dashboard to open the garage. When he'd driven in and switched off the engine, he turned to her. 'If you were going to ask me, don't. It's one thing to save your father's bacon, but I'm not going to ride to your boyfriend's rescue as well.'

He pushed open the door and got out, but before he could come round to the passenger door, she was standing on her side of the car facing him, her cheeks hot with colour. 'Pat is not my boyfriend!'

'I was using the term loosely.'

'And I didn't have any intention of asking you to help him.'

'Good.'

'He wouldn't have dreamed of suggesting it, either!'

Kynan inclined his head as though keeping an open mind on that.

'What's the *matter* with you?' Briar exploded.

'Nothing. I'm not the one raising my voice,' he pointed out.

Frustrated, she stalked ahead of him to the house. While she was still searching for her key, he had his out and had unlocked the door, standing aside for her to go in first. Casting him a look of exasperation, she found him looking utterly cool and self-contained, and checked a desire to throw her bag at him. He was right—he wasn't the one losing his temper, and maybe she was just being oversensitive.

She went straight to the bedroom, dropped her bag on the bed, kicked her shoes under it and pulled off her jacket. Going to hang it up, she felt the weight in the pocket and fumbled the package out. She crossed the room to thrust it into a drawer, just as Kynan entered, holding a glass half filled with what looked like whisky.

She closed the drawer, then shut herself in the bathroom and bent over the basin to splash cold water on her heated cheeks. As she patted them dry with a hand towel, she glimpsed herself in the mirror over the basin, her eyes darkened and unhappy, her mouth soft and vulnerable.

Deliberately, she made her lips firmer before returning to the bedroom.

Kynan was bent over the dressing-table, straightening abruptly as she appeared. Placing his emptied glass on its surface, he turned and said, 'Finished in there?' And with one hand in his pocket he strolled past her, closing the bathroom door behind him.

Briar stood staring at the drawer where she'd placed his present. She went over and opened it. The parcel was still there, sealed as she had left it. He hadn't been spying, had he? Perhaps he'd guessed it was for him, and was one of those people who couldn't resist peeking at presents meant for them? She shook her head. Surely Kynan was past such childishness. She took the parcel out and **buried** it beneath her sweaters in a lower drawer, then went into the kitchen to start dinner.

*   *   *

Kynan opened a bottle of wine, but Briar had only a half glass. By the time they'd finished the meal he'd drunk the rest. She wondered how much alcohol he'd had before leaving the bar. It wasn't like him to drink a lot, but the amount he'd had didn't seem to be affecting him.

Later he read the paper in the lounge and, after handing it over to her, took a folder from his briefcase and, balancing it on the arm of his chair, began making notes in it.

Seeing he wasn't in a talkative mood, Briar watched the news and a couple of TV dramas before switching off the set.

Kynan closed the folder, then got up and poured himself a glass of brandy, offering her one that she declined.

She felt compelled to ask, 'Why were you in that bar?'

He glanced at her as he sat down with the brandy glass in his hand. 'I gave a lift to someone who lives near there—his car's in dock. He offered to buy me a drink and I accepted.'

'You've been drinking a lot tonight.'

'Is that a complaint?'

She had nothing to complain about. As far as she could tell he was rock-sober. 'Did you have a bad day?' she asked.

'No worse than usual.' He paused, then said, 'Isa came to see me.'

'What about?'

'She wants to marry her property developer. But my father's will provides her with a generous income only if she doesn't marry again. She's asking for my help to break the trust.'

'That's a bit of a cheek, isn't it?'

He gave a slight, sour grin. 'Isa isn't short of that. I'm only glad she didn't approach my mother.'

'Can you help?'

'Maybe. In the event that she remarries the capital in the trust is supposed to revert to the family. If we waive our claim she may be able to persuade a judge to decide in her favour.'

'Isn't Nolan Cross a rich man?'

'Reputedly. Isa says she doesn't want to be entirely dependent, financially.'

'I can understand that.'

He shot her a look, then took a sip from his glass.

'Are you going to waive your claim?' Briar asked.

'It isn't up to me. I'll have to talk to my mother and Madeline.' He put down his glass and switched on the television again, saying, 'There's a late programme I want to watch. Why don't you go to bed? Don't wait for me.'

It was a clear hint that he didn't expect to make love to her tonight. Briar bade him goodnight and went to bed alone. She was awake when he slipped in beside her hours later, but she kept her eyes closed and he didn't attempt to touch her. She lay tense and still until his deep, even breathing told her he was asleep.

CHAPTER ELEVEN

ON HIS birthday Briar gave Kynan a card at breakfast before he left for work, but saved his present for later when he wouldn't be in a hurry.

'How did you know?' he asked, reading the card.

'Your birth date was on our wedding certificate,' she reminded him, although she'd been too keyed up that day to have thought of memorising it.

'Clever girl. Thank you.' He got up and came round the table to drop a kiss on her lips.

'Actually,' she confessed, 'your mother mentioned it.'

He grinned. 'I must go. See you tonight.'

'Don't be late,' she cautioned him, following him to the door. After he'd gone she returned to the breakfast-table and was surprised by a sudden dizziness. Sensibly, she made herself some toast and tea and sat down to have it before tackling the dishes and the housework.

She spent the afternoon preparing a very special dinner for five. When Kynan arrived home he sniffed at the aroma from the kitchen and said, 'Smells good. What are we having?'

'You'll see. Want a drink?'

'I'll freshen up first.' He headed for the bedroom.

When he came back, having changed into casual trousers and an open-necked shirt, she was waiting for him, a bottle and two glasses on the coffee-table, along with his present freshly wrapped in gift paper.

Taking the drink she'd poured for him, Kynan stared at the parcel, not taking his eyes from it as he sat down. 'A birthday present?'

'Didn't you guess? Pat helped me choose it. I mean, I bought it from him.'

'Yes. No, I didn't guess. As a matter of fact, until this morning I'd completely forgotten about my birthday.' He drank some of the wine and put down the glass. 'May I open it?'

Perching herself on the arm of his chair, she said, 'I wish you would.'

He peeled back the paper carefully, and opened the box. 'Very nice.' He lifted out one of the cufflinks to examine it. 'Wonderful workmanship.'

'Pat said they're not mass-produced.'

He replaced it in the box. 'Should we have gone out to dinner so I could show them off?'

Briar laughed. 'Not when I've spent the afternoon cooking. But you can put them on, if you like. Don't bother with a tie.'

'Want to do it for me?' He held out the box, and she slipped on to her knees in front of him and fastened the links into his shirt cuffs.

He bent forward before she could get up and, taking her head between his hands, tipped her face to him and kissed her mouth, his lips moving passionately over hers.

The doorbell pealed, and he muttered a curse and said, 'Who the hell's that?'

Briar pulled away from him. 'I'll go and see.' She smoothed her hair as she stood up.

All three guests had arrived together, and when she ushered in his mother, sister and brother-in-law, he cast her a wry glance before stepping forward to greet them with, 'I guess Briar plotted this.'

The evening went without a hitch, except for a moment when Madeline came out to help Briar serve the sweet she'd made, and found her clinging to the counter, her face white.

'Briar! Are you OK?' Madeline put an arm about her. 'Can I get you something?'

'No, it's been happening off and on all day. Something I ate, probably. I'm OK now.' She lifted her head, and pushed her hair away from her face.

Madeline said, 'Your colour's coming back. Could you be pregnant?'

'I don't know yet. I'm slightly overdue, but I didn't think morning sickness started so early.'

'It can. I was sick for eight and half months with Duncan,' Madeline told her gloomily. 'Better see a doctor and get a test.'

'Isn't it a bit early for that?'

'You could wait a week or two, if you like. But they can tell pretty early these days. Here, you sit down for a minute and I'll fix the sweets.'

They were sitting around drinking coffee and liqueurs when Kynan said to his mother and sister, 'There's something I have to discuss with you. I guess now's as good a time as any.'

As they looked at him enquiringly, he said, 'It's about Isa.'

Involuntarily, Briar asked, 'Is this the right time——?'

'There isn't one,' he assured her grimly.

His mother's lashes flickered, and her shoulders went very straight. Madeline put down her cup with a bang. 'That bloody woman! I thought we'd finally finished with her!'

His mother said, 'What is it this time?'

Kynan explained, his voice quite expressionless, and Madeline said, 'Madam Bloodsucker's never satisfied, is she? Surely Nolan Cross can keep her in the style Daddy accustomed her to?'

Mrs Roth said calmly, 'I want nothing to do with any money that came via Isa. As far as I'm concerned she can have it.'

Kynan turned to his sister.

'You're too good,' Madeline told her mother. Then she shrugged. 'But I certainly don't fancy another court case, and Mum's been through enough. I'll go along with whatever she decides. Can't you get Isa to sign something so she can't bother us again?'

'I could try,' Kynan said. To his mother, he said, 'Are you sure you want to waive your claim?'

'I'm sure,' she said. 'It's only money, and I couldn't possibly touch it, anyway.' She took a deep breath. 'If Calder wanted her to have it, leave it with her.'

Kynan paused, then said as though he felt obliged to point it out, 'He only wanted her to have it so long as she didn't remarry.'

A tremor of remembered pain crossed Mrs Roth's pale face. 'I know he ... felt very strongly about her. But that really wasn't fair of him. He couldn't expect to hold her beyond the grave.'

Kynan's mother was a remarkable woman, Briar thought. She could understand why Madeline and Kynan were so hostile to Isa. It must have been galling for them to lose their father to a woman like Isa. She couldn't help thinking that Kynan's father had shown an appalling lack of taste.

As if echoing her thoughts, Madeline said, 'I *still* don't understand what on earth he saw in her!'

Her mother gave her a tremulous smile. 'Sex is a very powerful urge in men. More so, sometimes, than love, or loyalty, or even honour.'

Madeline snorted, and Kynan gave his mother a searching, wordless look. His jaw clenched, and Briar thought a hint of colour came into the skin over his cheekbones.

When they'd gone, Madeline and David having insisted on helping to clear the dishes, Kynan turned back from the front door with his arm about Briar's shoulders. 'What have you been saying to my sister?' he enquired.

'She told me to look after you.'

'I didn't imply that you weren't,' Briar assured him. 'I suppose it was just a general remark.'

'She's grown fond of you.'

Have you? she wanted to ask him, but the question died before it was uttered. 'I like her, too,' she said instead.

'That's good.' They entered the lounge, and he steered her to the sofa, turning to the bar in the corner.

'She's very forthright, isn't she? Doesn't mince words.'

He looked around and smiled, obviously aware of what she meant. 'Maddy's intensely loyal, and she hates Isa.'

'Do *you* hate Isa?' Briar asked.

'Hate her?' He seemed to consider the question, carrying two balloon glasses of brandy across the room. 'No. She does have a way of setting my teeth on edge, though.'

'That's why you've never been able to see Laura properly, isn't it?' Briar diagnosed.

He frowned down at her, handing her a glass. Then he sat beside her, letting his arm rest along the back of the sofa.

'You keep her in Isa's place.' Briar added huskily. 'And me.' She was on dangerous ground here. 'Well, it's true in my case,' she admitted. 'We both know I...married you for your money. But it's not true of Laura, and you've no right to tar every woman with the same brush.'

His eyes had hardened, narrowing on her stubborn face.

Refusing to be intimidated, she went on. 'Just because Laura looks like a dizzy blonde, and acts like one a lot of the time, you've decided she's another Isa. And she's *not*!'

'But you are?' His intonation was odd, his gaze heavy as he studied her.

Briar bit her lip. 'How well did you ever know Isa, really? You had one holiday with her when you were a teenager!'

'The most unforgettable holiday I've had.' His mouth twisted.

Watching the expression in his eyes turn to a bleak distaste, Briar felt a hollow foreboding. 'What happened, Kynan?'

He stared broodingly into his drink. 'I grew up.'

A half-formed suspicion crystallised in her brain. Feeling sick again, she asked, 'Isa? Did she—help?'

He looked at her, saying with soft mockery, 'I'm surprised at you, Briar.'

She flushed, but didn't back down. 'What happened?' she repeated.

'She didn't seduce me. Oh—I was certainly attracted in my callow seventeen-year-old way. When she was younger Isa still had a kind of innocence combined with that lush and obvious sexuality, something irresistible to most men. My father had fallen for it, and in the throes of adolescence I was hardly proof against it. I spent three whole weeks in an agony of frustration, embarrassment and excitement. I *wanted* to hate her because she'd broken up my parents' marriage, but instead I was dreaming about her, spinning wild fantasies of making love with her, and racked with guilt because of it.'

Briar swallowed. 'How terrible for you.'

He looked up at the ceiling for a moment, then returned his attention to her. 'Not as terrible as it was for my father. One minute she was all over him, sitting in his lap, nibbling his ear, and the next she'd be stroking my arm, gazing into my eyes, telling me how tall and mature I looked for my age, and teasing me about my non-existent girlfriends.' He paused, a cynical, remembering smile on his lips. 'I was totally confused.'

'You don't think she was trying to make your father jealous?'

'Maybe. Perhaps she suspected he was already regretting leaving my mother for her.'

'Was he?'

Kynan shrugged. 'I don't know. He didn't seem exactly happy, but he was sexually very much involved with Isa. He couldn't resist touching her, watching her. And she was a natural tease. If she wanted to make him jealous she certainly succeeded. Before I left there was a major row. He accused us of cuckolding him.'

Briar drew in a quick breath, and Kynan gave a bitter little laugh. 'Of course I was righteously indignant that all that virtuous self-control of mine had apparently been for nothing. And scared witless.'

'You?'

Kynan gave a faint grin. 'I was barely seventeen. And my father, who'd never raised a hand to me in my life, was threatening to smash my face in. I really thought he was about to do it.'

Briar shuddered.

'Isa screamed and wept and told him he was crazy if he thought she'd look at anyone but him. The odd thing was, when everyone had calmed down, I felt that they'd closed ranks against me. Perhaps she was afraid she'd queered her pitch with him. He was, after all, a very wealthy man who'd already discarded one wife.' He took a deep breath. 'I was leaving the next day, anyway. They went off to bed and a passionate reconciliation—the walls were thin and it was torture listening to them—and I was left feeling more guilty than ever, and somehow terribly forsaken.'

Appalled, Briar said in a hushed voice, 'It must have been like losing your father all over again.'

'Yes.' He swirled the brandy in his glass and gulped some down. 'I've drunk too much. I'm getting maudlin.' He grimaced.

'Not maudlin,' Briar said. She felt this conversation was important. 'Did you ever tell your mother what had happened?'

'I've never told anyone until now.' He looked at her searchingly. 'Don't pass it on.'

'Of course I wouldn't.' She hesitated. 'He did leave you the business.'

'Remorse, perhaps. He had a go at patching things up over the next few months, in a half-hearted way, but I didn't want to know. Youthful pride, I suppose. Maybe I could have been more . . . understanding. He must have been a very unhappy man at the end.'

He seemed to deliberately shake off his mood, then. Turning to her with a strange look in his eyes, he said, 'You're very loyal to your stepmother. I believe it was more for her sake than your father's that you...married me.'

'You're probably right.'

He seemed to be studying her very carefully. 'Do you ever regret it?'

Briar lifted her chin. 'No, I don't regret it. Do you?'

'Why should I? I got...exactly what I wanted.' He moved his arm from the back of the sofa and touched her hair, lifted it back from her cheek. His hand went to her shoulders, easing her towards him, and he pulled her into his arms.

A few nights later, as they were clearing up after their evening meal, the doorbell rang, and Briar went to answer it.

Isa stood there, wearing a tight-fitting suit with a very short skirt and a low-cut jacket. 'Hullo there!' She walked in uninvited, forcing Briar to step back. 'The bride, herself. I didn't catch your name last time we met. Perhaps you don't remember me?'

'I do remember, of course. I'm Briar. Is Kynan expecting you?'

'No, dear. But I have to see him. You don't mind, do you?'

It wasn't up to her to mind, Briar decided, only she didn't think Kynan was going to be pleased.

She ushered the unwanted guest into the lounge and found Kynan already there.

'Isa wants to see you,' Briar told him. 'I'll leave you to talk.'

But as she made to pass him and go on to the dining-room, he caught at her arm, bringing her to a halt beside him. 'I'm sure Isa doesn't have anything to say to me that you can't hear.' Turning to the other woman, he said with cold courtesy, 'Sit down, Isa.'

When she had, tucking a leather clutch bag down beside her, he seated Briar and himself on the sofa and said, 'I did say I'd phone you when I had some news.'

'I know, but I was passing and I thought——' Isa gestured with her hands '—I'd just see how you were getting on. It's a social visit, really.' She smiled at them both, but Kynan's face was stony. 'You could tell me if you're getting anywhere, though.'

'As far as the family's concerned you're welcome to the money,' Kynan told her. 'I have my lawyer working on it now to see if it's possible to change the terms of the trust. As soon as there's anything definite I'll let you know.'

Isa looked faintly surprised. 'Your mother didn't object?'

Kynan shook his head with a hint of impatience.

'Well, well.' She gave a musical little laugh. 'I suppose she thinks the money's tainted.'

'Possibly,' Kynan said shortly. 'She doesn't want it, anyway.'

'How nice to have so much that you can say that.'

Kynan said very softly, 'I think we had better leave my mother out of this conversation.'

Glancing at his face, Isa blinked. 'Sorry. I didn't mean to sound nasty.'

'Didn't you?'

With a flash of temper, Isa said, 'You never could give me the benefit of the doubt, any of you! You've always hated me—even when you were just a kid and your father had that silly idea in his head about us.' She tossed her head. 'As if——!' She turned to Briar. 'Sorry, dear. I'm sure you don't want to listen to family squabbles.'

Kynan said, his face tight, 'But it wasn't so silly, was it? You had me so wound up at the time that he might well have been right. If I'd acted on my natural impulses——'

Isa turned back to him and said sharply, 'You'd have got your face smartly slapped!'

Kynan threw back his head and laughed.

Briar, with her eyes on Isa's face, saw her shrink back in her chair and grow pale before she shot to her feet, her hands clenched. 'You can laugh,' she said, her voice rising, 'but it's true! I never looked seriously at any man but your father.'

Kynan had stopped laughing, and was regarding her now with austere disbelief. 'He was hardly cold in his grave before you were throwing yourself at anything male that moved.'

Briar murmured, '*Kynan!*'

Isa's eyes widened, and her lips trembled. 'You don't understand!' she said. 'Have you any idea how much you look like him? That day you came—I was still in shock from Cal's death. All I wanted was comfort. I didn't really care about losing the judgement. I don't know why I even bothered to fight the will, except that somehow I felt I had to keep everything of him that I possibly could.'

Kynan made a scornful noise, and Isa flushed, her hands making agitated little movements. 'All right,' she said. 'The truth is I was still jealous of your mother. Of all of you. I was angry that he hadn't left everything to me, because it made me realise that all along he'd put you—and *her*—first, not me. I was just—a mistake. Something on the side, but it got out of hand because I wanted more than he'd bargained for.'

Kynan said flatly, 'Yes.'

Isa flinched, and Briar felt a quick stirring of sympathy.

'I wasn't crying because of the money!' Isa cried, rushing on in the face of Kynan's patent scepticism. 'That was only a...a sort of symbol. The judgement made me finally admit to myself,' she continued bleakly, 'not that I'd lost him, but that I'd never really had him. Not the part that mattered. And when you took me in your arms—for a little while it was like having him back.' Tears spilled from her eyes and ran down her cheeks. 'I know it was wrong of me, and crazy. I *was* a bit crazy, at that time. I didn't know how I was going to live without him. It wasn't really you I was... It was *him* I wanted! You were a—a substitute!' She wiped her cheeks with red-tipped fingers and, catching the stricken expression on Briar's face, appealed to her. '*You* understand, don't you?'

Briar nodded. 'Yes. I think I do.' Beside her, Kynan sat rigidly silent.

'I was madly in love with Cal,' she confided to Briar. 'That's something that none of his family ever cottoned on to.' She sniffed and fished in her bag for a hanky, wiping her nose and mascara-smudged eyes. 'Maybe I did set out to have him, and yes, I knew all along he was married. I was no angel. But it takes two, you know.' She looked at Kynan again. 'You think I was the one who did all the running? Look—I was twenty-one years old, and he was thirty-eight. You think I trapped him into falling for me—into marrying me? Hasn't it ever occurred to you that if he'd been happy I couldn't have taken him away from his wife?'

Kynan got to his feet, staring at her as though he'd never seen her before. His mouth was tight, his face pale and taut.

She took a step back from him, balling the damp handkerchief in her hand, and her mouth twisted. 'Well, you'll be glad to know that Cal lived to regret it. I spent sixteen years with a man who didn't love me. Have you any idea what that was like?'

She turned to Briar. 'I hope you two have something going for you besides sex. Men think it's enough, you know, but it isn't. Not without love. The trouble is, half the time they don't know the difference. And when they find out, it's too late.'

Kynan said, 'Are you in love with Nolan Cross?'

'No.' Isa cast him an almost pitying look. 'But I love him. And he loves me. It isn't what I had with Cal, but it'll be more...comfortable. You won't understand that, either, I suppose. Briar might.'

Briar thought of Laura telling her much the same thing, and said, 'Yes.'

Isa spoke to Kynan. 'You ought to hang on to her. She could teach you a thing or two about love and what it means.'

'She has,' Kynan said, making Briar shoot a surprised glance at him.

Isa gave them a strange little smile. 'You've got more to learn.'

'I'm sure I have.' He sounded oddly polite, and Isa looked at him searchingly, then gave a breathy laugh. 'Well, I guess that's cleared the air a bit,' she said. 'I don't expect you to believe a word I've said. You'd rather blame me for the whole mess. I suppose it's understandable. He was your father, after all, and I know you adore your mother.' She held up her hands at Kynan's quick scowl. 'All right—I'm not saying any more. I'm sure the lady's a saint. I apologise for still being jealous of her.' She stooped and picked up her purse. 'I guess I'll be going. Let me know about that other thing, won't you?'

'Yes,' Kynan said woodenly. 'I will.'

He went to the door with her. Watching them from the living-room, Briar saw him open the door and stand back for Isa. Isa hesitated on the threshold and looked back, and unexpectedly Kynan bent and kissed her cheek. 'Goodnight, Isa.'

Isa raised a hand and touched his jaw, stroking her fingers along the line of it. 'You do look like him, you know,' she said sadly, and gave his cheek a pat. 'Goodnight, Ky.'

Briar was still in the doorway when Kynan walked slowly back towards her. She stood aside and he passed her, then in the middle of the room turned to ask, 'Did you believe her?'

'Yes. Don't you?'

Without answering, he went to look out of the window. His back was straight, his hands thrust into his pockets. Watching him, Briar didn't think he was even seeing the darkened view outside.

At last he said, 'I suppose she's right. If he was trapped it was because he wanted to be. The blame was at least equally his.' Without turning, he added, 'And she was right, too, about him not really loving her. When I was staying with them he was still obsessed with her, but even then he must have begun to realise what he'd done in dumping my mother for her.'

'Your mother is an exceptional woman.'

'She's also a very proud woman. I suppose . . . but for that the marriage might have survived. My father was having a mid-life crisis, and Isa seemed made for the classic extra-marital fling. But once my mother knew about Isa, that was the end of the marriage.'

'Does it help to know they weren't happy?'

Kynan shook his head, turning to face her. 'No. I've never wished Isa ill. I just wished she wasn't there—in my father's life. I don't think it ever occurred to me that she was genuinely in love with him.'

She'd seen what a shock the idea was to him. It must have altered all his long-term assumptions about Isa and about the brief, fraught time that he had spent with her and his father. 'You've never been able to see her clearly, have you?' she said. 'Without a lot of emotional baggage from your teenage years getting in the way.' It had even skewed his view of Laura, because of some superficial resemblance of circumstances, and to some extent of herself. Perhaps he would come to realise that, in time.

'I guess,' he conceded, 'Isa can't help the way she is. Her sexuality is as natural to her as breathing. Back then I'd never met anyone like her. I don't think my father had, either. Maybe that's why he fell for her so heavily. She just naturally comes on to every male in sight.'

Briar said, 'I don't think she regards it as sexual—it's simply her way of relating to men of any age.'

He nodded. 'Perhaps she *would* have slapped my face if I'd made a move on her,' he admitted.

'I'm fairly sure she would. She'd have been shocked. To her you were just a schoolboy—and the son of the man she loved.'

Kynan frowned and rubbed a hand over his hair. 'I suppose I was hazily aware of it even then. I was still strenuously resisting the idea of my father being in love with a woman who wasn't my mother. And in spite of my physical response to Isa, I just didn't want to give her the benefit of any doubt on a moral plane.'

'It was easier to think of her as a grasping little opportunist?' Briar suggested.

Kynan's shoulders hunched. 'It made everything nicely simple. Black and white.'

'Things seldom are like that. Every situation has its shades of grey.'

'Including ours?' He'd been staring at the carpet, but now his eyes met hers.

Briar's breath caught. She'd been unprepared for the switch to a more personal level. 'I...guess so,' she agreed.

Still standing half the width of the room away from her, he gave her a slight smile. 'Don't look so wary. I'm not accusing you of anything. In fact——'

'What?' she asked, puzzled by the brooding concentration in his face.

'What do you suppose Isa meant when she said you could teach me a thing or two about love?'

Suddenly breathless, Briar said, 'I don't know. What did *you* mean when you said that I had?'

'Can't you guess?'

Afraid of coming up with the wrong answer, Briar wordlessly shook her head.

She thought he was weighing what he was about to say, his expression carefully masked so that she couldn't tell what he was thinking. She saw his throat work as he swallowed. His jaw clenched. Finally he said, his tone quite impersonal, 'Maybe it's time we put an end to this "infamous bargain" of ours.'

CHAPTER TWELVE

FOR a moment Briar couldn't speak. When she did, her voice sounded strange. 'What do you mean?'

'That's what you called our marriage, once,' he reminded her. 'Remember?'

Her mouth dried with panic. He wanted a divorce? *Now*? 'But...you can't!' she said. '*Why*?'

'Let's say that Isa has opened my eyes to what can happen when one person loves and the other doesn't. They were both desperately unhappy in the end. I wouldn't want that to happen to...to us.'

Briar felt the colour rise in her cheeks. He knew, then. He knew that she loved him. And because he was unable to love her in return he was offering to set her free.

She loved him all the more for that, although it broke her heart that he didn't feel the same. But she wasn't going without a fight. 'It's different for us,' she said, struggling against terror. 'We weren't in love when we got married. It was how you wanted it.'

'Oh, yes,' he said. 'I was very clear about what I wanted, wasn't I?'

'You said you intended it to last. That you wanted to have children.'

'I said a lot of things——'

'Well, you are!' It was probably unfair and if she'd thought about it she might never have told him, but she felt she was battling for her life. 'At least I think you are. I—I'm fairly sure I'm pregnant.'

She was quite unprepared for his reaction. He stared at her while the colour drained from his face. Then he closed his eyes and said, 'Oh, dear God—no!'

She should never have told him. She swayed on her feet, feeling sick. It crossed her mind that maybe Isa, long ago, had told Kynan's father she was pregnant, a desperate bid to get him to leave his wife and marry her. It was the oldest trick in the book, and she despised herself for using it to bind Kynan to her. 'Never mind,' she said huskily. 'It doesn't matter. I'll deal with it.'

She made to leave, intent on getting to the bedroom, because she really needed to lie down. The room seemed to be slowly revolving about her, and the sickness in the pit of her stomach kept coming in waves.

She was almost at the door when Kynan's hand fell on her arm, wrenching her about. The colour had returned to his face and his eyes blazed. 'Of course it bloody matters!' he growled. 'And what do you mean, you'll deal with it? It's my child, too! You don't mean to get rid of it?'

'. . . rid of. . . ? No!' Briar shook her head vigorously, but that was a mistake. The room stopped swaying and disappeared in an ocean of darkness. She was vaguely aware of pitching into it, and then of strong arms picking her up and a voice cursing in her ear. Then nothing until she found herself lying on their bed, with a damp cloth on her forehead and Kynan's voice saying, 'Briar? Briar!'

'Yes,' she whispered, because he sounded worried, and she wanted him to know she was all right.

'OK,' he said. 'Lie still.'

She had no intention of doing anything else, and the instruction struck her as rather funny, so that she gave a thin, wavery little smile.

Something brushed lightly—warmly—against her lips. 'I'm going to call a doctor,' she heard him say.

She managed to lift a hand, fumbling for his sleeve. 'No. I'll be all right...in a minute,' she murmured.

She felt her hand taken in Kynan's firm one, and curled her fingers about his. 'Truly,' she said.

When she was sure it was safe, she opened her eyes, and found him sitting on the bed beside her.

'Thank God,' he breathed, his fingers tightening on hers.

'It was only a faint,' she told him. 'See, I'm fine now.' She began to sit up.

Kynan pushed her back. 'Stay there. Did I frighten you that much?'

'It wasn't your fault,' she said. 'It's a common symptom.'

'Of pregnancy?'

'I shouldn't have told you,' she said. 'Not then. It wasn't fair.'

'Fair? What are you talking about? You'd have had to tell me eventually. How long have you known?'

'Only a little while. I haven't even had a test, yet. But I'm pretty sure.'

He looked down at their joined hands. 'Briar...I should have offered you your freedom earlier. Now...this alters things, you realise that?'

She swallowed, remembering his shock and dismay when she broke the news. He'd changed his mind again, and she was damned if she was going to accept being a wife under sufferance. 'I don't know,' she said, with a stirring of anger, 'why you should be so upset. You told me that you wanted me to have your children!'

He stood up, releasing her hand. 'You don't mind?'

'Mind? I don't understand you! I thought it was what you wanted!'

'I did! But——' He stopped, making a despairing gesture with his hands.

'But what?' Joltingly, a thought struck her like a blow in her midriff. It wasn't altruism that had led him to offer her a divorce. Not when it was followed by that extreme reaction to the news of her pregnancy. 'There's someone else, isn't there?' she asked painfully. 'You've met someone, and you want to get rid of me and marry her. It's her children you want, not mine.'

For several moments Kynan stood like a statue. Then, with a thunderous scowl gathering on his face, he said bitingly, 'Is insanity a symptom of pregnancy, by any chance?'

When she blinked at him in total noncomprehension, he asked, 'How could there possibly be anyone else, when you must know I'm totally, irrevocably, crazily in love with you?'

Briar was afraid she'd misheard. Had he just said he loved her? 'No!' she croaked, her eyes wide and disbelieving.

He flung out a hand. 'What the hell did you think I was saying out there,' he demanded, 'when I offered— God knows how I made myself do it—to let you go?'

'That...you knew I was in love with you, but you couldn't return it,' Briar told him.

'What?' He shook his head in fierce denial. 'You told me you're not,' he said flatly. 'You said I couldn't buy your love.'

Some emotion began spiralling inside her, at first slow and cautious, then singing and triumphant. 'And you can't,' she told him. 'But I can give all my love to you if I like. Free, gratis, for nothing.'

She watched the dawning comprehension in his eyes, and told him, 'I said your money couldn't make me say the words. I thought when you asked me to say them...that was all you wanted. Just the words, without any meaning. And I wouldn't cheapen my love that way.'

'Why in the name of heaven would I ask you to say it if you didn't mean it?' His eyes burned with furious hope. 'What use would *that* be?'

'I thought it was a power-game that you were playing with me.'

'But...didn't you know?' He sounded stunned. 'You must have known I loved you.'

Her heart beating suffocatingly, she said, 'How could I? You were so careful to spell out the terms of our...agreement. I didn't see the word love mentioned anywhere in that document I signed.'

He winced. 'I'll tell the lawyer to tear it up,' he promised, his voice shaking. His face was taut with something that looked almost like pain.

Briar held out her hand to him. 'Would you trust me that much?'

He took her hand again in a crushing grip and knelt at her side. 'I trust you with my life,' he said. 'It's taken me too long to recognise it, and I fought it like crazy because—oh, because of all kinds of stupid things. But I think now I must have loved you from the first moment I saw you coming down those stairs, looking like the goddess of my dreams.'

'No,' she said, laughing at him. 'That was lust.'

'That, too,' he agreed coolly. 'But I knew you were special, even then. So special I was afraid to admit how much I wanted you—not just in my bed, but in my life.'

'Afraid—you?'

'I'm an emotional coward,' he confessed. 'Haven't you realised that yet? I was scared of giving any woman the power to hurt me, or to wreck my life. Scared that I could be fooled by a pretty face, a shallow sexuality, a temporary madness, as my dad was. Every time I've met a woman who attracted me, I was able to remain in control. Why are you looking like that?'

'I was thinking,' she said. 'Madeline said something the same.'

'She did?'

'She told me you had trouble with intimacy.'

He grimaced. 'I guess you could put it that way. I'd never allowed myself to fall in love, never got out of my depth. The feelings you aroused in me terrified me. I was determined to remain in charge of my own destiny, and of my emotions—not to be like my father. After that first meeting I tortured myself alternately with doubts of your integrity and fantasies of making love to you. Every time I saw you I felt myself being drawn in deeper, and I'd tell myself it was the last time. But after you refused to speak to me any more, I went through several kinds of hell. I knew that for better or worse I had to have you. But more than that, I had to have your love.'

Watching her eyes widen, he gave a short laugh. 'When you asked for my help I was caught in a dilemma. I could have given you the money unconditionally, but then how could I ever have asked you to marry me? If you said yes I'd never know if a sense of obligation had made you accept. It didn't bear thinking about. So I came up with a solution that allowed me to neatly side-step the issue of my feelings for you, because I still didn't want to call it by love's name. Instead, I offered you a cold-blooded bargain, nothing to do with anything so dangerous as love.'

'Dangerous?'

'I told you, I was scared. Even after I admitted to myself that what I felt for you was love, nothing less, I wanted you to be the first to say it. I thought when I bought the house for you that you'd know how I felt without my having to say the words.'

'And I shied away from them, too,' Briar said softly.

'Yes. So I was more determined than ever not to let you know how I felt. By that time, I couldn't see a way out of the emotional minefield I'd made of our marriage. I thought what a fool I'd been, blackmailing you into marrying me. How could you love me when I was such a perfect swine?'

'You're not!'

'I certainly acted like one. I'd been greedy and grasping and utterly selfish, taking a gamble with your whole life and future because I wanted you so much. That was unforgivable. Isa was right. I've only just begun to learn about love and its many implications. I never in my life thought that I'd have cause to be grateful to her, but somehow that struck home. A whole lot of things suddenly became clear. I knew then that I had to let you go. You deserved the chance to love a better man than me.'

'I don't want a better man. I want you.'

He dropped his head and kissed her fingers. 'When you told me you were pregnant,' he said, 'my first thought was, She can't leave me now. I'm the father of her child. I felt like a condemned prisoner with a last-second reprieve. Then I began to feel sick at my own selfishness. I thought, I've left it too late, I should have freed her before. Briar—when I think of what I've done to you—what I've taken from you——'

'You've done nothing to me, and taken nothing that I didn't want you to,' Briar said clearly. 'Will you stop this breast-beating and come here and let me love you?'

She moved over in the bed, and he gave an unsteady laugh and lay beside her, looking down at her face. 'Are you sure you want to? Don't you have to be careful?'

'We will be,' she said, hooking her arms about his neck. 'Won't we? Kiss me,' she ordered huskily.

He didn't immediately obey. Instead he stared down at her face, studying its contours as though committing them to memory. 'I said I'd let you go,' he said, 'but when it came to the crunch I don't know that I wouldn't have come tearing after you to drag you back.'

'You wouldn't have had to,' she said, a smile on her lips. 'I'd have come back willingly—if you'd managed to get rid of me at all.'

'I do love you,' he said. 'So much.' And he lowered his head and kissed her.

Briar wound her fingers into his hair, and her parted lips welcomed his, their breath mingling. When their mouths left each other, she said, 'That wasn't so difficult to say, was it?'

'Not difficult at all. You're going to get sick of hearing it.'

'Never,' she said. 'You can say it as many times as you like.'

So he said it again, between kissing her and stroking her body, and helping her out of her clothes and impatiently shucking off his, and then he said it several more times, and heard her whisper the same words to him, before even those beloved, timeless words became inadequate for their feelings.

MILLION DOLLAR SWEEPSTAKES (III)

No purchase necessary. To enter, follow the directions published. Method of entry may vary. For eligibility, entries must be received no later than March 31, 1996. No liability is assumed for printing errors, lost, late or misdirected entries. Odds of winning are determined by the number of eligible entries distributed and received. Prizewinners will be determined no later than June 30, 1996.

Sweepstakes open to residents of the U.S. (except Puerto Rico), Canada, Europe and Taiwan who are 18 years of age or older. All applicable laws and regulations apply. Sweepstakes offer void wherever prohibited by law. Values of all prizes are in U.S. currency. This sweepstakes is presented by Torstar Corp., its subsidiaries and affiliates, in conjunction with book, merchandise and/or product offerings. For a copy of the Official Rules send a self-addressed, stamped envelope (WA residents need not affix return postage) to: MILLION DOLLAR SWEEPSTAKES (III) Rules, P.O. Box 4573, Blair, NE 68009, USA.

EXTRA BONUS PRIZE DRAWING

No purchase necessary. The Extra Bonus Prize will be awarded in a random drawing to be conducted no later than 5/30/96 from among all entries received. To qualify, entries must be received by 3/31/96 and comply with published directions. Drawing open to residents of the U.S. (except Puerto Rico), Canada, Europe and Taiwan who are 18 years of age or older. All applicable laws and regulations apply; offer void wherever prohibited by law. Odds of winning are dependent upon number of eligibile entries received. Prize is valued in U.S. currency. The offer is presented by Torstar Corp., its subsidiaries and affiliates in conjunction with book, merchandise and/or product offering. For a copy of the Official Rules governing this sweepstakes, send a self-addressed, stamped envelope (WA residents need not affix return postage) to: Extra Bonus Prize Drawing Rules, P.O. Box 4590, Blair, NE 68009, USA.

SWP-H395

HARLEQUIN®

PRESENTS Plus

"Virgin or wanton?" Oliver Lee is suspicious of everything and everyone.... When he meets Fliss, he thinks her innocence is an act. Fliss *may* be innocent, but the passion Oliver inspires in her is just like raw silk—beautiful, unique and desirable. But like raw silk it is fragile....Only love will help it survive.

Ben Claremont seemed to be the only man in the world who didn't lust after Honey's body...but he asked her to marry him anyway! Honey wasn't in love with him—so separate rooms would suit her just fine! But what on earth had she gotten herself into? Were their wedding vows based on a lie?

Presents Plus—the Power of Passion!

Coming next month:

Raw Silk by Anne Mather
Harlequin Presents Plus #1731

and

Separate Rooms by Diana Hamilton
Harlequin Presents Plus #1732

Harlequin Presents Plus
The best has just gotten better!

Available in April wherever Harlequin books are sold.

PPLUS23-R